Going Home

New life, new beginning

Kim Parker

Going Home

Chapter One

'**I**s this how we measure our life?' Sarah asked.
Beth turned to her friend; her pained expression evident as she allowed her body to sink into the tattered armchair in the corner.
She gently touched Sarah's hand '*... now that's a sobering thought*' she mused. '*Do you know many of them?*'

Sarah sighed slowly and surveying the room once more, realised most were familiar, a few she knew, but as for family and friends … well they made up a small percentage of mourners.

The room was filled with acquaintances and her partner Steve had boasted at having too many of those. In fact, he was quite brazen about it, claiming he only had friends when they wanted something. Sarah did not share his cynical view on life and held dear her friends.

But today she was facing a new reality and the most difficult part was that she was finding out about a man she had given nearly 20 years of her life to and realising she didn't know him, quite as well as she thought?

Burying him today had not been part of their 5, 10, 15- or even 20-year plan!

When they met, they were young and fell in love very quickly. Steve an enthusiastic writer, hoping for a big break, who also played the guitar and loved his weekends away on the road with the boys, playing at different gigs around the country. *'Why don't you get a hobby?'* he suggested, but when Sarah explained she didn't have the freedom he enjoyed, he would scoff, as if it was just an excuse for her to avoid trying something new.

They rowed, especially when money was tight, as the only money coming into the house was from Sarah and the rent and bills took care of that. Sure, they had a joint account, but Steve only put in *'what he could, when he could'* (his words) and when he was published *'life would* be ...'? ... well, no need to surmise anymore.

It's only with the benefit of hindsight that Sarah could see how foolish she had been and although believing in someone and helping them succeed with their dreams is what you do for love, it does tend to leave you a little out on a limb when the dream is over!

Steve's Mum, Jean, lived nearby and doted on him; her only son. Sarah had been thrilled that she met a man who loved and respected his Mum the way Steve did and Jean had welcomed Sarah into her heart and home from the start. Having lost her own Mum, Sarah welcomed the warmth of a family and it was very easy to feel safe and loved within it, so by way of giving something back, she supported Steve, emotionally and financially.

She taught in a school for most of her adult life, something she had a passion for and thought her future was mapped out. The demands of the role, along with the work required outside of school hours, with planning and marking, had given her very little free time so she had to admit sometimes it was easy to see how Steve had filled his life without her – on reflection so many things could have been different.

He would often sit up after Sarah had gone to bed and her early starts got even earlier with meetings before class. When the weekend finally came around Steve would accept a booking that Sarah felt was not worth the money, when you consider travel, petrol and often accommodation. It was too much of a sticking point to discuss time and time again so arrangements rolled over, month after month.

That said, during the week Steve would prepare dinner for them, arranged flowers cut from the garden and occasionally a laundry load made it to the washing line. Making it off the washing line and into the ironing basket was a stretch too far, but he was charming enough that he usually won the day. On the whole Sarah felt life was good – good man, good job, with the potential of better things to come, when success came knocking.

Maybe deep down she always knew … it's only the few who make it big, writers and actors and the like. But loving someone enough to be the one behind the scenes, well, that showed courage and commitment and Sarah never doubted her love for him.

Today though, was about goodbyes *'end of an era'* Steve's best mate Dan said at the church and it was evident that Dan was visibly struggling today. His wife Lois stood loyally by his side, talking quietly into his ear as he sipped the last of his drink, then looking at his watch, suggested it was time to make a move.

Beth offered Sarah her wine, but she declined. *'Hopefully we can head home ourselves soon'* she whispered. Sarah glanced up at Beth, who was now resting on the edge of the armchair. *'This IS a miserable turn out'* she whispered.

'He didn't work Sarah, so I guess he had no colleagues, like you or I?' Sarah raised her eyebrow and gestured a nod. *'I guess not'* she accepted.

The room was taking on a different feel now with most well-wishers having left and a few outside having a smoke or a last walk around the room, saying farewell.

In fact, it felt a little more light-hearted with laughter and storytelling, connecting Steve for the most part but also personal experiences surrounding bereavement, including funeral costs! Thankfully Sarah had included life insurance in her list of bills so at least that was one part she could stop worrying about. *A future without Steve*? Well, that was something she would think about tomorrow.

Steve loved a drink, and his parents too and although his Dad's demise had been drink related, the only time he would accept the '*haven't you had enough darling*?' was when he'd only had a couple. After that, Sarah may well have not bothered. From there on he was argumentative and unkind and this lively character became difficult to be around and Sarah knew to keep her distance.

'*Who's that?*' asked Sarah. Beth looked over to the kitchen door and watched as Steve's Mum tried to usher a woman outside. The two friends looked bemused, then Beth offered to find out.

Folk were still coming in and out so even between the living room and the kitchen Beth was stopped with well-meaning words of support to be passed on to Sarah, but eventually she made it to Jean who was clearing bottles and glasses.

'*Who was that*?' remarked Beth.

'*Who*?' asked Jean, while she busied herself, obviously trying to avoid Beth's question.

'*The woman you were talking to*' Beth pressed.

'*Oh, a neighbour*' came her dismissive reply.

'*Neighbour?*' Beth was now intrigued. '*If she knew Steve, she'd be welcome? Sarah doesn't know half the people here today*'

Jean continued to clear away and the two were interrupted a couple of times by passers-by coming in from the garden or those leaving, to say a final goodbye.

Beth glanced back towards Sarah who mouthed '*What's wrong?*' but Beth could only shrug her shoulders, eventually returning to her side.

'*That was odd*' she decided. '*Said she was a neighbour?*' Sarah looked puzzled too.

'*A neighbour?*' she echoed.

'*Maybe? ...*' Beth began. '*I mean, it's her house ... maybe she felt the neighbour had the nerve to show up at her son's funeral, uninvited?*'

Sarah looked past the animated bodies and noticed Jean on tiptoes, trying to see into the garden, her view slightly blocked by smokers outside.

'*No*' Sarah decided as she rose from the chair. '*I would know if she didn't get on with a neighbour?*'

Sarah headed for the kitchen, but Jean spun her round and pulled close.

'*How are you doing my love?*' a tear falling down her cheek. Suddenly Sarah was reminded of their shared heartache and Jean losing her only child? The two women held each other momentarily.

Now both childless – Sarah wondered if, to have loved and lost was the crueller position? As much as Sarah had dreamt of having a family one day, she never knew the loss of a child or the joy of watching them grow into an adult, loving their very existence, only to lose them later on.

'It's nearly over Jean' she whispered.

More voices called goodbye and only a few bodies now remained. Sarah realised Beth was missing but just as the thought crossed her mind, Beth reappeared.

'Where have you been?' she asked but Beth looked paler than usual. Her auburn hair and porcelain complexion started to flush a little with colour as she stepped inside. Her breathing exaggerated.

'err, car parking situation' she replied.

Sarah stopped her in her tracks *'Seriously, what's wrong*?' Out of the corner of her eye Sarah noticed the woman who had been in the kitchen walking away and realised Beth must have seen her.

'Who is she?' she asked once more, then her voice a little firmer pressing Beth into a reaction. *'No messing, I can't take anymore today – no more bull, just tell me'*

Beth was aware of Jean in the distance, standing

between the kitchen and living room door and now her hands were cupping her mouth and she was whimpering.

Her tiny frame looked small and fragile with the fear of what Beth was about to expose.

'*I think she was an ex*' Beth managed to say but Sarah knew her too well so continued to insist on more information. Catching Beth's glance behind Sarah spun round to see Jean, emotional, lowering herself onto a stool nearby. Beth took Sarah's hands and gestured they follow suit.

'*She said she had been in a relationship with Steve for about 8 years ….*' Beth wasn't even sure how she was getting the words out, but she knew she could hear the emotion in her own voice and if she could have avoided her friend being hurt any further today, she would have.

Sarah's eyes widened as she listened carefully, occasionally looking to Jean, realising this was not news to her.

'*8 years?*' she repeated, then again with a lowered voice, she mumbled '*Steve was seeing someone else for 8 years?*'

'*He loved you Sarah*' shouted Jean in a desperate bid to hold on to the girl she had loved and nurtured these past 20 years. '*He was yours … he never left you*'

Suddenly the room divided, a few walked out to

the garden and a couple of onlookers stayed quiet. Dan took Lois' arm and gestured they leave but Sarah saw him move towards the door *'Dan, did you know*?' she cried out. *'Dan? ...'* Standing up abruptly she called after him once more *'Is this true*? *Did you know?'*

For a moment time stood still and Sarah realised the secret had taken its toll on Jean as she was sobbing as her sister tried to comfort her. Ultimately, she was protecting her son's secret, his relationship with Sarah and the fallout from pain that would have destroyed any family – she was not condoning it, just looking out for them all and on the last day, when she must have thought she would no longer have to keep the secret, the truth outed itself.

Sarah's beloved mum had passed away a few decades ago when she was only in her twenties, her best friend and the loveliest mother to walk God's earth. She could never have forgiven Steve for such a betrayal and Sarah knew both their mothers would have struggled with the lie, but there was no strength like a mother's love.

Sarah studied the four men who played in Steve's band, their eyes desperately trying to avoid hers and looking to Dan for explanation.

Dan and Lois had been in their lives for a very long time. Steve and Sarah were Godparents to their girls. There had been many sleepovers, celebrations and so many cosy dinners together, discussing dreams and future plans. Dan stood still – Lois however? ... well, her reaction was one of surprise. Her eyes did not look away from Sarah until finally she turned to her husband for a firm denial.

Dan surveyed the room and noticed Jean being escorted into the garden, now Beth, Dan & Lois were alone. He sat down, let out a huge sigh of exhaustion and relief, then spoke softly and calmly.

'I think they met at a gig in Manchester' he said, *'I honestly did not know he was seeing her until a few years ago'.* He ran his sweaty hands through his hair, then placed them back on his knees. Lois lowered herself in disbelief beside him.

Sarah tried desperately not to cry aloud as she knew if she broke at this point Dan would stop talking and today was the day to know *everything* – she needed every bit of strength to help her get up tomorrow.

'He said it was over' Dan continued, *'that if I said anything ... even to Lois'* he clasped his wife's trembling hand *'it would get back to you and what had been a stupid fling would end his relationship 'his world'* he said'

Leaning forward Dan placed both his hands over Sarah's, begging her to understand his predicament.

'A lot of people held a secret to save my feelings' she mumbled and withdrew.

Lois looked to Sarah *'I'm so sorry Sarah'* she cried *'But I'm grateful I didn't know as I couldn't have hidden that; you would have known by just looking at me'*

Dan passed his wife a tissue. *'You know how close they were'* Lois pleaded and at the same time she stroked Dan's forearm reassuringly, but he never raised his head.

Beth placed her arm around Sarah's shoulders *'How did she find out Steve had passed away*?' she asked, but he only shrugged his shoulders and shook his head *'Not from me'* he said.

Sarah turned towards Jean who was walking back to the room.

'I know how hard this must have been for you Jean and he put you in an impossible position, but what about me?' Sarah started to weep, *'What about my feelings? My life of supporting him – if he hadn't have died, would I have ever known*?' By now Sarah's voice was getting louder, pain and frustration detected in her tone. She glanced between the faces she knew so well who tried not to engage; they carried their own regrets.

'What a wanker!' snapped Beth. *'Sorry, but he was*!' Beth squeezed Sarah a little harder *'You did everything for him Sarah and he was never going to succeed at anything. He was just happy that you looked after him and then this?'* Beth stood up and picked up her coat, *'Sarah, let's get out of here – you owe these people nothing!'*

Dan raised his head and along with Lois and Jean, she looked to each of them before she managed a very quiet tearful response. '*Wait*' she said. '*Please Beth, stop. I'm so tired right now, I can't think*'

Gaining strength Sarah rose from her chair and with Beth immediately behind her she wiped a tissue across her face.

'*I welcomed Steve's family and friends into my life, my home and I became part of yours, yet I was not given the same consideration?*' Sarah moved towards the hallway and before leaving the room she added, '*I never had the family I wanted, and you let me love yours – I deserved better?*' Beth tried to encourage her friend away, but she pulled back once more. '*My loyalty to him cost me everything, the one thing I always wanted was a family of my own and you knew that … to be a mother … it's all gone!*'

Lois tried to say it was never too late, but Sarah's cries were the only audible sound to be heard as she headed up the stairs to Steve's old room.

Even though they lived nearby, Steve's room had always remained available to them both and occasionally he crashed over and these past few weeks leading up to the funeral, Sarah and Jean had taken comfort from each other by being together.

She pulled a bag from under the bed and started throwing clothes on top, grabbing wash items with such force that a few things fell to the floor and Beth retrieved them.

'Come to mine' Beth begged *'Please Sarah, come back with me?'*

Sarah paused for a moment and slumped on the bed *'No, I need to get away ... on my own – please, I know you mean well Beth, but I just need to get away right now?'*

Leaving the bedroom felt final, not that burying Steve or trying to say goodbye wasn't final but anyone who has been through grief will know, it takes a long while for that to feel real. You go through emotions but it's all much the same each day whilst your head and heart deal with the practical side of living and your mind drip feeds the pain into quantities you can digest.

Sarah pulled the door and walked back down the stairs towards the front door with Beth in tow, armed with her coat and a small holdall.

'Jean, I'll be in touch and don't concern yourself about the rent. I will pay to the end of the month but you'll have to give notice to cancel the tenancy for Steve; I'm not even considered next of kin! I have no rights to the place; I was only good enough to pay for it!'

Jean was sniffling into her tissue. Dan, Lois and Jean were close by as Sarah and Beth left the house together, the door closing with such force behind them.

By the time they had walked just a short distance anger had kicked in and Sarah found herself cursing Steve and saying it was a good job he was dead as she would have left him and where would he be then, eh? Beth kept alongside and agreed with every sentiment, including Sarah saying she was going to take the life insurance and *'blow the friggin lot!'.*

At the end of the close, Sarah pulled out her phone and called a cab. Against Beth's better judgement and pleading, Sarah squeezed her friend tight and whispered thank you for being there for her during the best and now certainly the worst times of her life, but she needed to go.

'Let me have some space Beth, I will be fine, you know I will' Beth was holding back her own tears but could see Sarah was adamant.

'Let me know you are ok, please?' she pleaded *'Even a text?'* Sarah promised.

Moments later the taxi drove away and Sarah couldn't help but look back to see Beth and the street fade in the distance.

This was it – the first moment of her life where she was truly alone? She did not know where she was going, what she was going to do, and suddenly the reality of being single was terrifying.

She had always thought herself to be confident and capable but since turning 40 at the beginning of the year her life had spiralled out of control. Her anxiety levels left her feeling nervous at times and doubting herself but she put that down to the fact that time was getting away from her and that if she was to live without a family, then what of the future?

That unsettled outlook was hard to deal with and Steve was always saying '*we will*' but '*right now it's this, or that*'. She had been aware of her biological clock ticking loudly, so it had left her to feel uneasy about putting things off, but now? Now she finds out that he had time for someone else and perhaps it was a blessing they didn't have children – leaving in a taxi with a family would not be so easy?

'*Where to love?*' the Cabbie enquired and for a second Sarah was unsure, then another prompt from the driver and she found herself asking for the Station.

Growing up Sarah and her mum would head to Cornwall whenever possible. Her Grandmother lived there so the three generations would have the most amazing Summers together and it was always a dream of her Mother's to return, but sadly she was taken early, another dream unfulfilled.

She had promised to keep in touch with her Grandmother but of course in the early years she was concentrating on her career and the old lady could see how determined she was, so encouraged her commitment. She asked Sarah to find time when a school holiday came around and although the two spoke on the phone, it would always delight her when Sarah managed a few days together.

Then sadly she passed, and Sarah had been truly alone without any family to call her own until she met Steve and the rest is history.

Now heading to the Station, it felt right to be going home.

The Station was always busy and heading to the ticket office Sarah realised it was late afternoon and she had no time to be indecisive.

This morning she had woken in Steve's old room, she thought she would be sleeping there tonight, her and Jean discussing the day and sharing stories; just supporting each other? Never did she imagine she would be leaving her behind at the end of an emotional day, heading off somewhere, completely alone?

One ticket purchased for the overnight sleeper from Paddington safely in her hand, Sarah felt the first moment of panic. '*What on earth was she going to do when she got there?*

Boarding the train however, triggered good memories – the sounds, the smells, something overly familiar transported her back to outings with her Mother and being helped on to the top bunk.

Sarah closed her eyes and let the memory flow through her veins. It brought a warm smile to her face and a warm tear to her eye. *'I miss you Mum'* she whispered. *'So much'*

There was a lot of noise outside; whistles blown and doors slamming.

Sarah placed her bags onto the top bunk which looked particularly compact now and closing her door, she locked the world out.

The train slowly shunted out of the Station and it felt like she was shedding her skin as she left the drama of London behind.

Exhaustion and fatigue were taking over now and before she gave in, Sarah text Beth to say she was fine and that she would call her tomorrow. Beth knew of her desire to return to Cornwall one day and knew she had talked it over with Steve through the years, but it had always been Beth's belief that it would never be the right time for him.

Steve used to say, *'one day'* and Sarah believed him, but he used to say they would start a family and that day never came either. Sarah curled up on the bottom bunk and held her pillow tight, not thinking she would ever be able to sleep, but she could fight it no longer.

Chapter Two

When the train pulled into the Station the following morning a cascade of noise announced their arrival and Sarah was surprised she had managed to sleep at all; her body aching, but she knew it was less about the small bunk experience and more about emotional stress. The memory of Steve was not far from her thoughts from the second she opened her eyes and welcomed the new day. His betrayal was so raw and try as she might she could not manage to put the information to the back of her mind.

This should have been a time for grieving, but her emotions were all over the place.

Eventually all passengers vacated the train and Sarah was swept along with the crowd, finally bursting through the exit and being welcomed by a brilliant blue sky.

The next memory washed over her in an instant with the gulls overhead and the smell of the sea drawn into her very core. She once again closed her eyes and soaked in the past *'Morning Mum'* she thought to herself. *'We're home'*

She made her way to the bus station and bought a ticket for the Cove, then sat excitedly by the window and watched as she recognised so many turns in the road and the craggy hillsides, enticing her back.

Stepping off the bus, the little town was empty due to the early hour, but ahead Sarah noticed a little café open for business, which was fortunate as the small holdall she was carrying felt a little heavier with each step.

The smell of bacon rolls wafted into the street as she pushed aside the heavy door. The waitress arrived and Sarah found herself explaining she used to visit the Cove as a child and the waitress followed with *'Yeah, it's one of those beautiful holiday places'* her smile, welcoming. *'You back for a holiday then?'* she inquired.

Sarah was smiling back at her, then found herself thinking about that before answering. *'A change of scenery'* she said, realising that she wasn't ready to offer any more. In fact, quite the opposite. She wanted to be herself, no pain or bitterness, taking comfort from a place she loved by the people who loved it with her – a healing that she could receive no where else.

'Morning George' the waitress beamed and went back behind the counter to serve the gentleman.

Sarah watched as the very well-dressed customer passed over his payment, then made his way to a window seat. As he passed by another, he handed them their utensils before making himself comfortable.

'George, are you trying to take my job?' she gig-

gled. George laughed back at her.

> '*Not at all*' he smiled. '*Gives me something to do*'

He was obviously well known as moments later a few more customers came into the café and they acknowledged George too; some offering a handshake and wishing him a good day.

Sarah rose from her seat and walked towards him '*Excuse me*' she announced. George looked up and gestured for her to take a seat, which she gratefully accepted.

> '*Sorry to disturb you, but I'm thinking you're a local and I could do with some advice?*'

George smiled, his tanned face and creased forehead were that of a happy man and she felt he would be a good person to ask. He continued to sip his tea, then moved his newspaper to one side, allowing her a little space.

> '*Do you know of anywhere to rent for the summer*? She began. As the words left her mouth, she realised that she did in fact have a plan after all – it would have been good to have known that an hour ago when she had hesitated at the bus stop.

> '*Firstly, you're not disturbing me*' George assured her. '*I usually breakfast alone so it's nice to have company*' he mused.

Within minutes they were conversing comfortably, and George was able to place memories for

Sarah, through the changing of the years, properties bought and sold and was excited to talk about the Cove and happy to enjoy the way Sarah remembered it.

'*More tea?*' the waitress interrupted, as she fiddled with their cups. '*There's a letting office in town*' she contributed.

Sarah looked up and realised she was trying to be helpful, but shook her head.

'*Thanks, but I'm thinking more for the whole summer*' Sarah lowered her eyes and fiddled with her own cup and saucer until the waitress retreated. Raising them once more she was met by George's curious stare, then reassuring smile. He was trying to read the situation, but being a gentleman, he continued their conversation before gesturing that they walk together and to Sarah's surprise, she agreed.

Outside George offered his hand to greet Sarah formally. She thanked him for his time, and he nodded saying once again that he thoroughly enjoyed her company.

'*I'm George*' he announced and Sarah offered her name by return.

'*Listen*' he said. '*I do know of somewhere you could rent for the summer, if you're interested?*' They continued together, passing a few shop windows on the way and George continuing to acknowledge passers-by.

'Yes please' Sarah enthused.

Relief flooded through her veins and perhaps a little emotion showed in her voice

'It's not much' George told her. *'Don't get too excited'*

'I just need a little time to myself' she said, her voice a little meek.

'Then I'm happy to help' George replied and indicated a turn between two buildings,leading down a narrow lane.

George advised Sarah to watch her step, remarking on the rain and how slippery the cobbles were, adding they were particularly dangerous when it snowed (but hopefully there wouldn't be much of that in the next couple of months). They shared a laugh.

As they reached the bottom, they were hit by the sea breeze, fresh before the days heat and the salty sandy dust tasted familiar on her lips.

'Here we are' he pointed out. Sarah stood in wonder. He was showing her a small beach house which had doors opening out on to the sand.

'George?' she gasped. *'That is so kind of you, but I really need a little space to myself and you have already done me a great kindness with your time'*

George held his hand up *'No, no … I don't live here'* he quickly replied.

'You don't?' blushed Sarah.

'No' George grinned. *'I have been known to sit here and watch the ocean, but it's been left un-attended far too long'.* George turned the key and went inside, inviting Sarah to follow him. *'I just can't bear to sell it'* he added, with a melancholy tone.

All his life George had looked after others, a life in service he said, but now he felt he had no purpose but to fill his time idly.

He smiled again whilst opening the curtains, then the doors to the veranda, George gestured for Sarah to come inside.

'Forgive the tears' Sarah said. *'I'm having a tough time at the moment and this is just amazing, so yes please … may I stay here for a while?'*

George nodded, then cupped her hands.

'You know Sarah' he told her. *'Life is full of interruptions, but my Mother used to say you can't know good, until you have known bad – otherwise you have nothing to compare it with?'* He tapped her hands. *'Let this summer be the good, eh?'*

'I love that' Sarah whispered, wiping a single tear from her eye. *'Thank you, George,'* she said and placed a kiss on his cheek.

'Well …' exclaimed George. *'Today is full of surprises!'*

For the next half hour George showed Sarah

around, saying he would return later with some fresh bedding and if she had any further questions or needed direction, he would go through things with her then.

She stood in front of the doors and filled her lungs with fresh sea air and recalled the last 24 hours and knew it was crazy that she had woke with a little trepidation first thing, having said goodbye to her first love, the prospect of facing life without him, yet here and now she was looking out to sea, feeling a little more at home than she had felt in a long time, unable to find any emotional link to the drama she had left behind. It was surreal.

So surreal, but this was her life now – new beginnings, meeting new people and allowing herself to understand her misgivings and ultimately trying to heal.

Sarah had loved Steve very much; in fact, he had been all that she had known as far as a loving relationship was concerned.

But in the last 5 years she could not deny their relationship felt one of convenience at times and she had voiced this to Beth when frustration with Steve got the better of her. She wondered whether she would have stayed with him if she had not been the financial support and Beth had asked her to consider her own feelings many times.

It fell on deaf ears and admittedly Sarah had private moments where she questioned herself, but loving Steve gave her the strength to continue, always banking on the future and the possibilities.

One of the last rows the couple had was particularly hard to forget, starting with Steve arranging a gig with the boys but being unable to support Sarah at a school function, one that he had promised ahead of time to attend with her.

He knew how important her job was to her and she rarely asked him for support, but an award was coming her way and she really wanted to him to share the moment.

He gave her the speech about earning when he could, but Sarah still asked him to turn it down, to be by her side this one time but words were spoken, and a heated argument ensued. Sadly, when Sarah felt desperate, she blurted out words that were never to be taken back. '*Wow*' he said, '... *so you want a man you don't love anymore, to be by your side at a work's do?*'

Sarah tried to take it back, but it was too late and when he started to walk away, he said something about them being on the same page which, of course, was even harder to hear, than say.

She also knew he had been caught out drinking heavily and drugs came into a couple of overheard conversations with the guys, '*recreational*' he told her but Sarah did not understand that at all and they had argued frequently. '*He finds money for that!*' she relayed to Beth, but once again she felt it not worth pursuing, just the realisation that sadly they were growing further apart.

When the call came to say Steve had been rushed to Hospital with a possible drug overdose, there was a split second when Sarah wanted to say to Dan that it was his own fault and he deserved it, but as Dan begged her on the phone to hurry, she placed the receiver down and walked to the door, making her way to the car with no sense of urgency.

Driving to a Hospital some distance away, to a town where he played his last gig, felt unreal. Not once did she think he would die?

When she arrived at the Hospital Dan fell into her arms and at that moment, that very moment, Sarah's heart skipped a beat; as Dan lifted his tearful face to meet hers, she knew …

Even when they headed back down the corridors, the Hospital deafening with sounds of emergency all around, bustling noises echoing the halls and people rushing past to get the job done, Sarah walked calmly and quietly to the room set aside for Steve.

Jean was already there, sobbing by her son's side and holding his hand, she called out to Sarah, where she clasped her hand and cried aloud.

Looking down at Steve's lifeless body, his skin mottled, she felt numb. Dan was trying to control his emotions and kept crying '*It was an accident Sarah, an accident'* but Sarah just nodded, unable to shed a tear.

'*What are we going to do Sarah*?' Jean was wailing but Sarah let go of her hand and stepped back before becoming a little lightheaded and encouraged to sit.

'*He did this*' she whispered, '*He did this to us*'

The beach was beautiful and Sarah watched as dog walkers made the most of the cooler air and a few families made their way along the sand to find their ideal spot to settle for the day. Further out there were a few smaller boats and the occasional cloud passing by overhead, but all in all, picturesque.

She looked around the room and rolling up her sleeves, started with the sofa, then the chairs, pulling off heavy covers and giving the cushions a good plump.

Working her way through the room and cleaning down the kitchen, before taking out the rugs for a good bash, helped clear her mind.

As promised George returned with bedding and could not believe how much Sarah had achieved in a couple of hours. He placed a tin on the table, along with tea, coffee, milk and biscuits then a few apples and bananas.

'*Thank you so much*' Sarah beamed, '*You truly are a life saver*!' George smiled and opened the tin to showcase some freshly baked scones.

'*I didn't make them my duck*' he beamed. '*They still look after me at the big house*' he explained and pointed to the white house, nestled high on the hill. Sarah followed his hand, '*That's beautiful*' she said. '*Is that the family you worked for*?' George rose from his seat and walked to the open doors, with Sarah beside him.

'*Yes, man and boy*' he replied proudly. '*over 50 years*' he confirmed and raised his chin, with shoulders back.

Sarah gasped, repeating '*50 years?*' – Suddenly her own 20-year life of service felt like she got off early with good behaviour!

George went on to explain how he had worked for the family and his Lordship had taken him on when his father was in service and his father before him. George had initially helped the gardener as a boy and worked his way up, with training offered by the family where he found promotion and became his Lordship's Aide.

Later he was asked to spend a little time with their two sons and helping with Charles and Jackson proved to be the most rewarding part of his duties and certainly something that made his face light up, '*his proudest moment*' he went on to say '*watch-*

ing them grow into fine young men'

'*Did you have a family of your own*?' Sarah asked. George broke his gaze away from the house '*No, sadly*' he explained '*We weren't blessed that way*' he said and with that he gave a huge smile as if to reassure Sarah he had reconciled himself with that.

Sarah apologised for being so forward. They had only known each other a few hours and to be asking such personal questions was not something she herself would appreciate just yet, but George again assured her it was absolutely fine to ask and in fact he didn't get the chance to talk about his life, or the family, so he welcomed the opportunity.

He went on to say he still saw the boys and the family still kept him in their thoughts; even delivering his dinner every day.

His Lordship had since passed away, but Lady Martha had been such a wonderful friend and he had been privileged to be part of something very special. His own wife had helped in housekeeping and that is where they met, and they were married for 39 years.

As their conversation continued Sarah found herself talking about her own life, explaining how she had just buried her partner of 20 years and George's eyes widened as his sipped his tea. He did not wish to interrupt her and perhaps could see that his new acquaintance could do with a friendly ear, something he was happy to offer.

'I found out the same day that he had been see-ing another woman for the past 8 years – all that time I had been supporting his dreams, his lifestyle and yet I didn't know he had betrayed me?!'

Sarah looked puzzled and her upset evident, so George explained how he believed life was a test, guiding us onto the next phase. He watched as Sarah took control of her breathing and wiped her eyes, agreeing with his wise words.

'He did love you' George assured her. *'You know when someone really loves you'*

He waited for Sarah to acknowledge what he had said and when she smiled and nodded her head a second time, he went on to say that he had loved two women in his lifetime, but only married once.

Sarah listened intently as he gave a little more in-formation than perhaps he had meant to, saying he believed it possible to love two people, but as Steve had stayed with Sarah, he knew his place was with her, adding he was his own man. If he had wanted to leave her for the other lady, he would have? He hoped Sarah could retain some good memories and see that we're all human, we make mistakes and we learn and Steve was no less of a good man because he found himself caring for two people.

A little later George left, and Sarah considered his words and found herself wondering whether he had loved two women at the same time, rather than one after the other as she had first thought? She had not intended to talk about her past, let alone to a stranger but George had been so kind, his words helped.

Even this lovely gentleman had been a young man once and she could see he was a thoughtful person and maybe to survive she needed to rethink her feelings and try to salvage some good from the years she had given to Steve. She had loved him, he had loved her but found himself being close to another and if she had been in the same position, what would she have done?

No ... far too early! *He was a two-timing knob (and that was that)!*

Sarah finished making the bed and finally it felt like a home.

Changing into a t-shirt and denim shorts Sarah pulled one of the armchairs a little closer to the doors and sat with her drink, just watching the world go about its business.

Calling Beth was difficult, in some ways by talking with her she was still reliving the past, leading up to today; a tie if you like to the drama, so she found herself keeping it brief and making excuses to end the call.

The second call was to her headteacher, who had proved a wonderful support when Steve had passed away and offered extensive compassionate leave, which at the time Sarah wondered if she would be best to take, but now she knew.

Thankfully the school holidays were only a few weeks away, so she agreed on early leave and sent a letter to the parents, followed by one to her class of girls to pass on good luck for the year ahead and wishing them an amazing summer break.

She told the head she would stay away for the holidays and return in a couple of months, but right now she needed to take stock of life.

To her surprise, as she was talking it over, she found herself listening to a little voice in her head posing the question?

    'Why go back?' but pushing that to the back of her mind, she finished the call.

A dog walker called out and Sarah woke with a jump. Not realising she had fallen asleep; she stretched her arms wide, before adjusting her position. It was also slightly unnerving to see just how close some of the families were to the veranda in front of the hut.

One lady raised her hand to acknowledge Sarah and she blushed as she waved back, wondering whether she had been snoring and cringed at the thought of sleeping soundly in view of everyone.

Finally, the beach began to empty and Sarah buttered herself a couple of scones. She could not face going out to find food and her body still ached.

Washed down by another cup of tea, Sarah stretched her legs across the small pouffe in front and let the cool evening air wash over her.

Chapter Three

It must have been very early in the morning when Sarah woke a second time; the sky was darker and the air a little chilly, so she pulled a small throw up to her chin and yawned.

There were no people on the beach now and the waves were strong, washing up onto the sand and pulling back with some force.

Sarah stepped outside, the veranda was cold and the sand coating the wood was a little damp. Looking to her left she could see a couple of lights inside a few beach front properties, but most were in darkness.

The big house on the hill was still visible and a little light near the edge was projecting a delicate glow to the front.

A wake-up shower and a change of clothes helped the day begin and Sarah realised it must be early so perhaps a little stroll along the sand before the world and his wife arrived, would be a good idea.

By the time she got back to the hut it was around 7am and Sarah unpacked the last of her bits and started searching through her phone for a little direction but by 8am George was knocking, hoping it wasn't too early and offering her bacon and eggs and an apology for talking too much the day before, which of course Sarah felt was unnecessary.

'It's lovely to see the place appreciated like this' he said to Sarah and looking around he credited her *'It looks homely'*. George was surveying and smiling and Sarah couldn't have agreed more, *'It is lovely'* she soothed.

'Did you sleep well?' George asked.

'Yes, I did and I'm surprised I did, though I didn't quite make it to bed' she giggled. *'I woke up in the armchair; the first time to see people staring at me from the beach and the second time, alone, in the early hours!'*

The two laughed and George pointed out to her

that she must have been exhausted and that he was happy he could do someone a good turn.

Sarah placed her hand on his forearm *'George, you will never know'* she said quietly.

'Right' said George firmly. *'I'll not hold you up any longer'* and with that he rose, but before he got to the door, he placed a local paper on the counter so Sarah could familiarise herself with what's on, which she was happy to accept – *'I had searched my phone but this is much better.'* She smiled.

Sarah thanked George once again and the two parted ways as she confirmed she would get cash first thing, but he told her there was no rush. He really did want to help her and money was not the incentive.

Looking in the mirror, Sarah pulled her wavy brown hair high into a ponytail and decided no make-up was required today; her complexion was pale and her eyes, tired.

Her shirt was tied at the waist and her ¾ denim jeans were finished off with a flat sandal. *'No-one knows me'* she thought.

Then, with her bag over her shoulder, Sarah pulled the door behind her and made her way between the buildings and back up the narrow lane.

Beautifully decorated boutiques were dotted either side and at the top, the lane opened onto the main high street.

It felt familiar, yet different and of course with the years in between that shouldn't have been a surprise. There were a couple of buildings that triggered memory and the old picture house was now a modern shinier version, advertising the latest blockbusters, '*perfect for a rainy day*' her Mum used to say.

There was the usual holiday shop, everything from flip flops, buckets and spades to a variety of tat for sale for holidaymakers to take home as a '*thank you*' to the neighbour for seeing to their plants or feeding their cat. How they managed to stay open year after year was a feat in itself?

Sarah said hello to a few faces along the way, smiles from families enjoying their time together and occasionally a workman trying to complete a job, but hindered by happy people getting in his way.

Towards the end of the street Sarah felt her excitement build as she was nearing the sewing shop her Grandmother had owned for many years and the little flat above, she called home.

The display window appeared smaller than she remembered and thinking back it used to be full of sewing patterns, wool and the obligatory dummy standing in the corner, displayed in such a way, so as to entice you in.

Sarah and her Mum used to pop in to see her Grandmother, make her a cuppa out the back and then let her know what time they would return; after a visit to the beach or nipping to town on the bus.

It was idyllic and Sarah smiled holding her hand over her heart as she entered through the rickety door.

Now the place was rented by a photographer and there were beautiful photographs on display, some framed for sale and others were from invited amateurs, who captured different views of the Cove.

'Hi there,' said the owner. 'Do you need any help?' The tall middle-aged man approached, then suggested Sarah look around, before she explained her Grandmother used to own the premises, something he said he knew a little about.

'I think it was empty for a year or two after that' he suggested. That seemed a shame she thought, thinking how loved it was by her Grandmother and then that was it, over. At least now it had been given a new lease of life and maybe quite fitting, it was showing the Cove to newcomers and enjoyed by those who remembered it fondly.

Looking at some of the photos Sarah was able to replace some of her fragmented memories and take herself back to a gentler time.

'I will search out some of the older ones' he suggested, as she browsed. 'I have boxes that were donated by locals, unwanted. There's bound to be one of the old place, around your Grandmother's time?'

Sarah couldn't help by showing her appreciation and gratefully accepted his kind offer, though she realised that would take up his valuable time.

'Forgive me for being so forward' she remarked cheekily *'but if it helps, I would be happy to spend time going through them for you?'*

'Greg' he said with a smile *'My name is Greg and you are?'*

Greg held out his hand. *'Sarah'* she enthused.

'I don't have time just yet Sarah, but bear with me and I will get some of the boxes down from upstairs over the next couple of days and you could take a look, if you want?'

'Really?' beamed Sarah *'That would be amazing … thank you so much'*

Greg found himself studying her, admiring her even, then got caught by Sarah who in turn felt a little uncomfortable. The last thing she needed was unwanted attention!

'I will pop by at the end of the week' she confirmed and even when turning to leave, she was aware Greg was watching.

On her way-out Sarah noticed an old street view so she bent down to take a closer look, rows of little shops and buildings in black and white – nudging more memory. Without any doubt she knew she was in the right place, at the right time and a slow intake of breath to relax her beating heart, confirmed it.

By mornings end the Cove had been covered and a few unexpected detours offered rare scenic views, some she had never seen before.

A couple asked if they could help her when she was looking for direction but for the most part, she spent a few precious hours on her own.

As lunchtime approached Sarah nipped to a small tea shop and bought a ham filled roll to take away and then made her way to the sea front where she sat down and watched the world go by. It was breathtakingly beautiful and if she had to choose anywhere in the world right now, she would not hesitate in choosing the Cove.

In the distance Sarah noticed George with a small shopping bag making his way down the street behind her and then he was out of sight. What would she have done if, not for George? It could have been so different, staying in a soul-less B & B. It was as if she was being guided, finding George was a twist of fate and she looked up to the sky and quietly thanked the universe.

On the beach below Sarah noticed a couple having words and then an ice-cream being thrown, followed by a dramatic stomp away. The woman, possibly in her 40s was having none of it! She marched up the beach, getting closer to Sarah, where she could nip through the gap between the bench and the locked gate that kept vehicles off the sand.

Seeing Sarah sitting there and trying to avoid eye contact, the woman huffed on by, then started muttering to herself as she headed down the street. Minutes later the victim of the ice-cream mugging took the same steps and made his way towards her. He had knocked the cone off his shirt, and it laid on the beach where it landed, but he was covered in ice-cream and when sweeping his hand across to clear it, he'd coated his hand. He was fuming.

He caught Sarah's eye, nodded the fastest '*hi*' and squeezed through the gap, calling after the woman as she headed off, with gusto.

Sarah finished her lunch and sipped her water, thinking to herself that relationships were just too much hassle right now – even something so minor as an argument was difficult to watch and for a 40-year-old such as herself, feeling alone suddenly felt quite liberating. She wasn't a widow as they never married, she wasn't even his next of kin for that reason, she was a singleton and that meant she was beholding to no-one.

'*Are you ok*?' Sarah stopped suddenly as she noticed a lady struggling for breath in the heat. The air was humid, and Sarah gestured to the bench. They slowly shuffled along together but each step seemed uncomfortable for the lady; her breath laboured.

'I have water' Sarah offered, as she pulled the bottle from her bag, placing it to the old lady's lips, which she gratefully accepted.

For a moment it appeared she was gaining her composure but then she clasped her chest and said she was in pain. Sarah tried asking about medication, but she could see her questions were not being heard; the lady had her eyes closed and the waves of pain were obviously too much to bear.

Looking about Sarah beckoned a few people and someone said they would call an ambulance, another said they thought they knew who she was and roughly where she lived but waiting for the ambulance felt like an age.

The Paramedics arrived and rushed to her aide, with a relieved Sarah tapping the lady's arm, telling her she was in safe hands and once the oxygen mask was placed on her face the old lady smiled and nodded, her frail arm raised slightly in thanks.

'You did a good job' the Paramedic praised. *'you didn't panic'* Sarah raised her eyebrows and said she wasn't sure about the not panicking part, perhaps better at disguising it?

His face was strong and his features rather attractive and doing an amazingly worthwhile job too – *for goodness' sake, it must be the heat!*

The ambulance pulled away and Sarah thanked those who had assisted her and for a few minutes they chatted until a little normality returned.

∞∞∞

Finding her way back to the beach hut was straightforward enough and it felt wonderful to be heading home. Somewhere safe and secure, where she could be herself and it occurred to her that she may stay longer. What did she have to return to? Jean would be a constant reminder of the deception and Beth, in all her loveliness, was a reminder of her old life and as for their friends, well … every time she thought about any of them, she wondered who else knew?

A huge sigh was expelled. '*Ooh, that bad, eh*?' came a familiar voice. George was standing in front of her as she headed for the beach hut door.

'*Hi George*' she beamed. '*Just helped an old lady with heatstroke, I think*' she explained. '*Anyway, she went off in an ambulance so hopefully she will be ok*' George followed Sarah inside '*Ambulance you say?*'

'*Yes, a passer-by called them and to be fair, I know it felt a while, but I guess it wasn't. Bless her*'

George handed Sarah a receipt book and said he would prefer to use that – he wasn't worried about money and didn't want her to either.

'*Well,*' he said. '*I will leave you for good this time*' he chuckled.

'*You're welcome anytime George; this is your home and you are my only friend, remember?*' Sarah teased.

'*Thank you, but you need your space and that's my place over there*' George pointed out the side window to a small bungalow in the distance with a flag blowing outside.

'*Drop in if you need anything my lovely, open all hours*' he finished and with that he winked and pulled the door behind him.

'*Ok then*' Sarah said to herself. '*My new life starts today*' but before she could walk away from the door her mobile rang and Dan's name appeared on the screen. A sharp pain hit her stomach and she stared at the words, accept or decline?

'*No, not today*' she said and picking up the mobile, she powered it down and dropped it into her handbag. '*Not today Dan!*'

The evening lent itself to a night of reflection. Tearful thoughts flooded her mind and although Sarah was able to see the joy in having somewhere to run to, it was true what they say: '*you can run, but can't hide'.*

Questions seem to be growing by the day; how could she not have known about another woman?

I mean, Steve would be home most evenings? She knew he visited the library during the day for research … was that when he used to see her? Did she live locally? Does she have a family and what did she think their relationship was or where did she think it was heading? Sarah kicked the pouffe hard, sending it a few feet away. '*you utter shit*' she cried.

The most frightening realisation was that she could have been with him for many years to come and for what? For him to leave her in the end? Or after he gained success? Would he leave when his options improved? She pushed hair from her eyes and slumped deep into the chair, letting its saggy bottom pull her down.

He used to tell her she didn't know him at all and at the time it was hurtful and of course she refused to accept that; in fact, quite the opposite she told him. The real truth was simply that due to his arrogance and argumentative nature, she used to let things slide – it wasn't worth the upset that followed. If she hadn't known him as well as she did, knowing when to choose her battles, it wouldn't have been worth investing in the relationship at all.

Now though … sitting alone in a different County, dissecting her choices, well perhaps he was right all along? She obviously didn't know him or what he was capable of? Loving him was one thing, liking him ever again, was questionable.

A shower and bed were the only things she could manage right and tomorrow she would have to see about getting food and supplies and then perhaps return a call to Dan.

Chapter Four

The following day started well. No alarm clock, just the morning light seeping through the curtain and to her surprise, it was already after 8am. Sarah felt refreshed and her body ached less, she thanked the soft bed and sea air for that.

Pulling on a summer dress and carrying her sandals Sarah stepped out onto the cool sand. It felt wonderful between her toes and the water was fresh as it met the shore.

'*Good morning*' came a call up ahead and as Sarah looked up, she raised her hand above to shield her eyes from the light.

'*Morning*' she replied and when closer she could see a bulldog bombing towards her. '*Look out*' he shouted, but too late, the bully barged into her legs and sent her flying. Sarah squealed, then laughed as she righted herself.

'*Sorry, sorry*' the man cried as he rushed to save her.

'*I'm fine*' she laughed, '*He's heavy!*'

'*Sure, is*' said the man '*He's a bruiser. I try to get him out before families start arriving; he knocks little kids over like skittles*'

Sarah laughed and bent down to stroke the beast. '*Wow, you're solid*' she smiled, and the man bent down to pat him too. '*Hugo, aged 5*' he said, and '*and an absolute knob!*'

'*You can't call him that*' Sarah laughed. Hugo ran around her legs and again knocked into the back of her causing her to stumble forward and lose her footing.

'*See*' he smiled, '*absolutely no sense!*'. The two laughed and chatted for a moment before he pointed towards her, '*Ambulance lady*?'

'*Sorry*?' Sarah looked a little confused.

'*We met yesterday*' he paused. '*the lady with heatstroke?*'

'*Ahh, the Paramedic?*' came Sarah's reply, then she stepped back and squinted in the sun before realising she did recognise him.

'*Are you here on holiday*?' he asked.

Sarah was smiling. '*Sort of*' she said. '*A much-needed break, but definitely for the summer*'

Sarah lowered her head a little and then bent down to stroke Hugo who had run back to the pair with a dirty stick. '*Oh no*' she squealed with delight '*No, it's disgusting*'

'*I'm Jack, by the way*' he said '*We may see you about, it's such a small town and everyone knows everyone, and everyone's business unfortunately*' He smiled the most amazing smile, his face lighting up and that attractive jaw line she noticed yesterday was evident today. Tanned with a strong brow and gorgeous eyes that drew her in.

'*Yes, may see you about*' Sarah agreed, then petting Hugo she said goodbye and continued her stroll, looking back as she walked away, Jack doing so too.

The beach spread out for miles ahead, the sea framing the edge, with the white cliffs and hillside adding a splash of colour and depth, it really was the most beautiful backdrop. Sarah drew plenty of deep breaths and let memory transport her to her happy place, familiar sounds and laughter in her mind when she thought of her Mum stepping in what she had thought was a shallow rock pool, only to find her foot (*and her favourite flip-flop*) disappear up to her knee. She fell back onto her bottom and try as she might, after pulling her mucky leg out of the bottomless hole, the flip-flop was lost forever.

They had walked to town barefoot so her Mum could buy a new pair but every time she tried a pair on, she decided they were not as good as the one she lost. Sarah welcomed such memories and they were so needed right now. *'Love you Mum'* she whispered.

Getting closer to the busiest part of the beach, Sarah made her way towards the stone steps and stopping to dust the sand from her feet, she slipped on her sandals and walked around the corner.

She stopped occasionally to look in windows but Sarah had never been one for shopping; girlfriends used to invite her to town, but she really didn't enjoy that type of day.

Through the window of one store, Sarah recognised another face – it was the ice-cream mugger; this time she was eyeing up some jewellery and a quick glance at the window had Sarah step away and move on to the next. But being a warm day and the doors wide open, Sarah heard the lady, *'Well he hasn't asked me yet, but I am expecting he will soon'*.

Sarah smiled and thought surely not a proposal. If she threw an ice-cream at me in public, there would be no way I would be looking to buy her a promise of any sort! Mind you, she realised, she was certainly no judge of character. In fact, if she had thrown the occasional dairy product, life may have been altogether different?

Further along there was a small supermarket, costing the earth but selling the basics, Sarah entered and picked up a basket. A few *'good mornings'* were exchanged, and Sarah made her way around the store, picking up items for lunch and some pasta for tea and then stopped to study the small selection of wine near the counter.

'Do you need any help?' the assistant asked.

'I'm just looking' replied Sarah. *'Not sure what I fancy and to be honest, I only have one glass, so it seems a waste, just for me'* She walked further along and placed the basket on the counter.

The young blonde assistant had her hair pulled back and Sarah couldn't help but study her piercings and tattoos, so much so that the girl grinned *'Yeah, I know. My Mum doesn't approve either'* Sarah put her hand in the air and tried to defend herself *'No, honestly, I don't dislike, I just thought … ouch!'* They chatted, whilst packing.

The youth of today were brave Sarah surmised, and although her students were younger, they had very definite ideas and opinions and unlike her, they set no limits.

They tried things, even if it got a negative reaction,

but that was acceptable. They had no ceiling, which was refreshing and she realised she could learn a lot from them.

In Sarah's day, you finished education, went on to further that, or got a job, but you didn't get a job, go travelling, then get creative and do a few other things before you decided what direction life was going to take you? There was something empowering about the courage to just give it a go. No fear or too much thought, just 'carpe diem'.

'I think it's great; young people go for it! …Good for you' she concluded and glancing at her name badge as she was leaving, she thanked Becky and wished her well.

Sarah made her way to the lane and slowly worked her way down. It had been wonderful to reminisce during a morning stroll and every hour she was here; she knew that she would find it hard leave. Again, the thought that home didn't feel like home anymore, was a real concern, but the Cove did.

Once inside the hut Sarah placed the items in the cupboards and fridge and settled down with the intention of returning a call to Dan.

She curled up on the friendly armchair as the sun warmed her face. Taking a deep breath, she talked herself into what she would say and tried to prepare for what Dan was going to say. Was she ready to hear a confession of a sort? He had time to think about his part in all of this and perhaps Lois had put pressure on him in the meantime and he may have come to the conclusion that he no longer owed Steve loyalty? Another sigh or two, then Sarah selected his name and dialled.

For a moment, no answer, then suddenly a gasp from Dan and a request for her to hold for a moment. Sarah waited, she could hear her own breath down the phone and now her heartbeat set the pace. Finally, Dan apologised and thanked her for calling back.

'*You, ok?*' he asked. His voice was soft, a little nervous and the familiarity of a friend was a surprising comfort to her. Sarah nodded, then realised she had been silent for too long, so found the strength to say she was.

'*Where are you?*' he asked but Sarah said she was away, needed a break and turned her thoughts to Jean.

'*She's beside herself*' Dan explained. Sarah interrupted him and found her patience snap '*is that why you called? Am I supposed to be worrying about everyone else ... still? Seriously?*' She dropped the mobile to her chest, another intake of breath and a muttering of unrepeatable words escaped, before managing to replace the mobile to her lips.

'*Sorry*' he hastily replied; his voice a little croaky with emotion, reminding Sarah that she called him.

'*I want to be so angry with him Sarah, I really*

do ...' he continued. '*He's gone, he hasn't got to worry about anything anymore, but you know ... he was my best friend and ... I miss him*' Sarah heard Dan clear his throat, trying to compose himself, then a sniffle and it was hard to hear. '*I get it*' she managed to whisper.

'*Lois is on my case*' Dan explained '*Not that I am looking for sympathy, I swear*' he was quick to add. '*She feels hurt by my not telling her on the one hand, but then pissed off with me that I didn't tell her as she would like to have told you, so you could make a decision about your own life ... then upset 'cos, if I can hide something like that from her, what else can I hide? ... oh, you know what she's like, it's got to her, that's all*'

Sarah was listening, her eyes closed and her head resting back on the chair. She felt childlike, curled up small, holding her knees close to her chest in a way of keeping it all together.

She listened while Dan explained how he had tried to reassure her and he knows the damage is done. He has also tried to be a support to Jean who feels she is grieving the loss of both Steve and now Sarah, leaving her on the same day.

Before the call began one of the thoughts Sarah had was that she would ask more about the mystery woman, her whereabouts and so on, but listening to Dan pouring out his woes and knowing that his marriage had taken a hit, she just couldn't face it.

In the end she was reassuring him that Lois needed a little time, she knew that Dan was a good one, he never blew up like Steve. Never used drugs and worked hard for his family, so he just needed to give her a little breathing space and let things settle.

She also found herself advising him that Lois could call her if it would help, but after she'd offered, she realised that this time away was for her to heal herself and not to heal someone else. Lois had Dan. Jean had her sister, and Dan too by the sound of it.

Before the call ended with Dan, he said he would talk with Sarah when she was ready and though it was of very little comfort, he would answer her questions. She made an agreeable sound and told him to take care, finishing off by asking him to let her know the date for the reading of Steve's will. She would return for that and to clear out the apartment, as soon as she could.

Dropping the phone into her bag, Sarah's heart swelled. This was never going away she thought. '*I want to wake up and it all be over*'.

∞ ∞ ∞

The afternoon was a slow one, with a lot of people watching, broken up by a few emails to notify suppliers that she no longer required services for the apartment from the end of the month. That felt strange as she was leaving herself nowhere to return to and Jean's was no longer an option!

It was hard to switch off and Sarah realised her mind was muddled, fuelled by sadness and frustration, grief and anger, hurt and pain, they were all there. She loved her job and the students she had seen grow and develop, she took huge pride in that but otherwise, no family, no home, no sense of direction?

She had already called about Steve's life insurance and at least that was not in question. Paperwork had been sent off and it was a relief to see that the Policy had paid out and she could rest easy on that.

It gave her peace of mind, knowing that when she decided where she would like to settle, she could afford to buy a small property and with everything else to worry about, it was the biggest blessing she could have asked for.

Trying to close Steve's bank account however was proving harder – originally Jean said she would go with her and they could sort it together. She knew he had no bills as such, but there were things he had signed up for and Sarah was adamant she would not be accepting responsibility for anything else!

As early evening approached and the beach emptied, Sarah found herself at a loss. Her thoughts turned to Beth. At the beginning she was an amazing colleague, then close friend and the one constant, positive, figure in her life and she could not have survived without her.

But Beth connected her to the past; she held no blame and had always been so considerate of her – sometimes getting in the way of Steve's outbursts but that did not phase the little red head at all!

On a night like this, the two would have chatted at length. It proved difficult to talk during the school day as they were based at different ends of the building, even lunchtimes were not scheduled at the same time due to teaching KS1 and KS2, so it often fell to the evening where the two would confide in each other and put the world to rights.

After talking with Dan, the temptation to speak with Gracie and hear her voice had subsided. She so wanted to support her friend and knew that she would be worrying about her in, but the strength was not there tonight and so a text of love and reassurance would have to suffice.

And tomorrow was another day.

Chapter Five

Waking up early, Sarah found herself a little emotional.

It was to be understood and although she realised that, today felt like a step in the wrong direction.

To her surprise, she missed Steve? Recent drama had not allowed for grieving and during her shower Sarah sobbed out loud, lowering herself to the bottom of the shower cubicle, wrapping her arms around her knees; the water cascading over her head and tender body.

'*Why?*' she wailed, '*Why did you do this to me? I can't love you anymore*'. Sarah lifted her face and let the water pound her forehead and her swollen eyes, gulping down water as it filled her mouth. She felt so lost and so in pain she could hardly breathe, then realised that she didn't care if she couldn't breathe, the water causing her to gurgle, then choke. Suddenly she stopped, spluttered and spat, then sitting abruptly, she corrected herself and her thoughts and gasped for air to fill her lungs.

By the time she had towelled herself dry and headed back to the bedroom she found enough strength to recognise how easy it was to give up, to feel the huge burden of pain and wondered how anyone managed to move forward when the past remained unanswered.

She got dressed and decided that she would get out in the fresh air and walk awhile, reminding herself that she needed to be strong, to get up every day and just deal with that day. That is what her Mum would have told her, and many times she had heard her say things like '*one day at a time*' or '*be gentle on yourself*' when she was comforting or supporting a friend. So, that is the advice she would take – today would be a walk on the beach, just to clear her mind of anything negative; as best she could.

Clearing breakfast things away and heading for the door, Sarah was aware of a shadow on the other side. She opened it to find the lovely George smiling back at her.

'*Too early*?' he asked.

'*No, just right*' she replied and stepped outside to join him. '*I was just going for a stroll*' she mentioned and gestured with her hand that he could walk that way with her, unless he needed to go inside, which he didn't.

'*Love to*' he said and the two stepped onto the sand, Sarah with her sandals in her hand and George now taking off his sliders.

'*I don't bother to wear socks now*' he told her. '*If I'm staying local, it's easier, otherwise the sand gets everywhere*'. He was smiling and just being in his company lifted her spirits.

George was an old soul she thought, warm on the outside with generosity and good heart and inside so knowledgeable and thoughtful, he knew what to say and when and he was surely heaven sent for Sarah.

Without any prompting from her he glanced up, then quickly away, seeming to understand she was low or maybe her reddened complexion confirmed it.

'*You, ok*?' he soothed. Sarah nodded. If she

tried to speak, she would cry and let's be honest, she only met him a few days ago and if she constantly blubbered when he was around, she would have no friends at all.

George started relaying a story and it continued until they were both laughing about the irony of the situation. Fifteen minutes later George showed Sarah the view from the Cove as it bent around the rocks, a most wonderful distraction and the two sat down on one of the largest boulders she had ever seen, to take in the view.

'*Breath-taking*' she said, so softly that George nearly missed it.

'*Sorry, I said breath-taking,* she repeated' This time George nodded in agreement, '*Sure is*' he agreed.

'*Anyway*' said George '*I said I would leave you in peace, I know, but I thought I would see if you fancied coming out with me this evening?*' He looked at her with a sideways glance, then decided he had placed her in a position, he spoke before Sarah had time to answer.

'*Honestly, it's not a problem and you did make it very clear that you were here to take some time out, so you won't offend me my love, that is never going to be the case, ok?*'

Sarah had only a moment to think about it and before she was ready, she heard herself accept his invitation. '*That would be lovely*' were the words that left her lips. She pulled back and said that actually she wasn't sure she was the best company today but George chose only to hear what he wanted *'Great'* he said enthusiastically. *'I will call for you around 7pm'* he said. *'May do you good to have a change of scenery'*

The joy in his face was evident and he appeared to be lifted by her acceptance. She could not deny how much he had done for her, so it was the least she could do.

Having thought a lot about her past these few weeks, one of the downsides had been to accept how much she did for everyone else and how little she did for herself, but today it was clear that she loved doing those things and being there for others. The buzz she got from being kind and helpful was something to be celebrated and the being *'too nice'* that Steve had often criticised her over, should be worn as a badge of honour!

　　'Where are we going?' Sarah asked and for a moment she hoped he wouldn't say the local bingo or something similar, but George pointed to the house on the hill where he spent most of his working life, *'Taking you to **my** home'* he said.

Sarah gasped with delight (and a little curiosity), *'Really*?' she grinned. *'Won't they mind?'*

George laughed, *'No, I have been invited and I asked if I could bring a guest. Just glad you said yes'*

　　'It's a date then' Sarah chuckled. *'Dinner will*

be lovely, I just know it will and having heard your stories, I can't wait to see inside'

George helped Sarah step over a little rock pool and the two continued towards the hut pausing by the gap in the fence.

Sarah wanted to see the photographer she had met previously and relayed her curiosity to George, with eager excitement.

'That will be interesting for everyone' George agreed. *'You won't believe how it has changed over the years'*

'I know' beamed Sarah excitedly, *'I can't wait'*

Nearing the end of the street George took his leave and said he would collect Sarah around 7pm, assuring her it was a casual invitation and to not worry about a thing.

She took a sigh of relief as George walked away and knew that once again, he had come to her rescue and a day that had started so desperately, had been enlightened by his presence, his company undeniably comforting.

Sarah pushed open the shop door and a small bell announced her arrival.

'Morning' she said brightly.

'Morning yourself' said the Photographer, quite happy to see her pretty face enter the premises.

'*How's the holiday going*?' he inquired as he walked towards Sarah smiling, his teeth so white Sarah looked away so as not to stare. Instead, she changed direction and pointed to a printed beach view on a stand, '*I love this, especially the black and white*' she added.

He agreed and talked for a few minutes about an upcoming photographer that he was helping; 'a local' he went on to say and his joy in seeing someone grow in talent was something to appreciate.

'*Did you find time to search*?' Sarah asked, her voice questioning, hopeful.

'*Come this way*' he grinned and walked ahead of Sarah, his white teeth glowing in the dark, as they took a small step into the back-office.

There in front of her was a table laden with photographs, most of them loose and on top of each other, with a few he had kindly displayed on a stand, slightly bigger in size and full of detail. There were also some framed photographs, tarnished by time, sitting on the counter but all were black and white, some dusty, but Sarah could not hide her delight.

'*No way!*' she squealed and stepped quickly from one to the other '*I can't believe how many you've found!*' she clasped the Photographer's arm and squeezed it which he very much enjoyed, '*You superstar!*' she exclaimed.

'*My pleasure*' he beamed. '*In fact, I've now

opened up other boxes and I'm going to display some of those next month. So many of the residents will remember the boat yard and the photos are incredible. I recognised some of the faces from when I was young, old Jake who made the nets for example; he was in quite a few photos and he died a couple of years ago so his sons will love them'. It was so obvious to see his passion and here was another stranger, re-living their life after meeting her. It felt quite surreal to know she was having an effect on others during one of her lowest times; everything happens for a reason she used to say and now she believed it.

Suddenly there was a familiar face looking back at Sarah and the Photographer held his finger on one photo, sensitively touching the lady's face. *'Recognise anyone*?' he asked.

Sarah felt a swell of emotion and clasped her hand to her chest *'Oh, thank you'* she whispered. With that, a little tear filled the corner of her eye and she swept it aside as she touched the photo tenderly. *'Hello you'* she sighed.

Standing at the front of her shop, her Grandmother was talking with a customer and another snap showed her giving a little wave to the camera, smiling; her apron wrapped around her body, her pockets filled to the brim.

The shop doorbell jingled once more and Sarah was invited to take her time.

Sarah spent the next hour in the shop, compiling

the smaller unframed photos to one side, as he said she could take them with her.

They were family memories and he only asked that she allowed him to keep a couple of the larger framed ones, so that he could arrange a *'return to the past'* exhibition, along with the photographs of Jake and other retailers he recently uncovered.

Then a moment of utter joy for Sarah as she found what looked like her Mum and her, standing near the shop front. Her Grandmother was slightly out of view but could be seen just inside the window and Sarah and her Mother were smiling at each other, Sarah with an ice-cream in one hand and a paper windmill in the other. She clasped the photograph close to her chest.

The Photographer was busy talking with visitors and occasionally Sarah's concentration was broken by a little laughter as their chatter grew. Finally, Sarah placed the chosen photographs in her bag and made her way back to the main shop.

'I cannot thank you enough' she said, holding the bag closely. *'This is more than I could have hoped for; you will never know how special this is for me'*

'Seriously, not a problem and as I said, it has opened up so much for me too' the Photographer walked closer, *'It's the age-old thing for any trades-man'* he went on, *'Always finding time for others but never for yourself. If you hadn't come along, I may not have got around to those boxes for some time'*

Sarah smiled gratefully *'Well, I'm thrilled I did then and your idea about showing scenes from the past will be amazing; I'm intrigued to see the old place come to life, but those who have lived here all their lives will be blown away!'*

Walking out of the shop, Sarah thought again about how her day had started and like a gift from heaven, she was holding precious memories, something she may never have uncovered if not for her return.

The rest of the day got away from her and back at the hut she placed the photographs on the kitchen table, then used her phone to take copies and sent them to Beth by WhatsApp where she received a speedy reply. *'No way - is that you*?' with a smiley emoji. Sarah chuckled out loud and returned a message back *'That's me!'* she replied, along with a love heart saying *'with my Mum'*

By the time the evening arrived Sarah was questioning whether she was up to socialising and with who?

Yes, George had asked her to accompany him, but he wouldn't be there alone, surely? It opened all sorts of questions and nerves and anxiety stirred in the pit of her stomach. If she hadn't wanted to be supportive of George, she would have opted out but that did not seem fair, all things considered.

She didn't bring too many items of clothing with her, it had been a bit of a rush so looking through the travel holdall, Sarah threw aside her jeans, leaving a few blouses and one special dress but it was too short for a dinner.

The other option was a simple summer dress that perhaps was a little low at the neck but made up with a little more length around the knee; it would have to do.

Oh well, no time now, she thought and got back in the shower for a freshen up, deciding not to wash her hair again, but lift it up instead.

The small red printed dress had a short sleeve and dipped down at the front to a daisy button and nipped in waist. She lifted out her Mum's locket and placed it around her neck before scooping up her tousled hair and tying it carefully with a loose ribbon.

Then out came the make-up, something she had not bothered with since arriving but tonight called for coverup; a boost of confidence.

Foundation and blusher along with a little eye colour and mascara, Sarah finally added a lip tint and did a quick pout, then smiled into the mirror. '*Oh boy*' she sighed to herself. '*What are you doing?*'

Thankfully and without any time to change her mind, the door tapped, and George's silhouette was once more to be seen.

'*Good evening*' Sarah announced as she pulled the door wide.

'*Wow*' George stepped back '*You're a show stopper!*' Sarah giggled, '*And you a charmer*' she said.

He offered his elbow and smiling Sarah accepted, taking hold of his arm as he escorted her back up the lane.

'*Are we walking?*' she asked nervously. George laughed, gave an emphatic no and pointed to the car in the distance '*Too far for me*' he announced.

As they reached the top, the door was opened by a driver who tipped his hat to Sarah and then shook George's hand.

'*Evening Edward*' acknowledged George, '*This is Sarah*'

'*Nice to meet you*' Edward replied, then closed the door behind them and their journey began.

Sarah wanted to pinch herself and told George that she couldn't believe how these past few days had helped her so much, that she had been so sad, yet here she felt like she could be happy again. George listened intently as she explained that meeting him by chance in the coffee shop had made all the difference; his generosity and kindness had given her somewhere to stay and he continued to be such a friend to her, that she would never be able to repay him.

George tapped her hand gently and reassured her that she had given him a reason to be those things – he had missed being there for someone, spending so much of his life in service, then to retire, but for what? He had no lady to share those lonely times with, money didn't fill that void either.

He explained further that even at his age, having a friend was special and it had been wonderful to hear a young person talk about the Cove that he loved so dearly and hearing her call it *'home'*.

Edward darted his eyes to the rear-view mirror, then away before guiding the car through the huge stone entrance.

He opened the door and assisted Sarah first, then George, and walked them to the stone steps leading to the front door. He wished them a good evening and said he would return them home when they were ready.

The building continued to unfold in front of them and now standing in front of its huge doors, it appeared to wrap itself around the curve of the Cove – its stature was magnificent.

George once again took Sarah's hand as they climbed the few steps and went inside, being greeted by a very well-dressed doorman who acknowledged George with fondness, then Sarah, offering to take her bag; she had no coat to give him so it felt rude not to let him take her small purse which he folded over and placed to one side.

'*Her ladyship will meet you in the drawing room*' the doorman announced, and a young lady escorted them into a warmly lit room, with a low fire glowing in the corner. However warm it may have been outside it was easy to see how this enormous room felt a little chilly, so the fire was a welcome addition.

'*Are you ok?*' George spoke with a parental tone.

'*Yes, it's all so beautiful*' Sarah whispered but he could hear in her voice she was a little nervous.

Looking round the room, there were numerous works of art on display, again their size more befitting to a museum. There were a couple of portraits that George explained were past generations and then he showed her one of his Lordship and Lady Martha. He was clearly proud to have been part of something special.

'*George*' came a welcoming voice. George spun round to greet Lady Martha as she walked towards the couple, her hands stretched out before her and taken readily by him.

George beamed and again his affection for the lady was very clear to see. He turned to Sarah and introduced her to her Ladyship, but nerves took hold and Sarah stuttered a little before remarking on her beautiful home.

'*It's a pleasure to meet you*' said Lady Martha as she made her way to a large seat near the fire, beckoning Sarah and George to join her, which they did.

'George has been telling me all about you and when he said you would be joining us tonight, I was honoured' she continued, smiling occasionally at George.

'I'm happy to be here' Sarah said. *'George has been so kind, and we only met a few days ago, so I don't know what I would have done if I hadn't met him'* Sarah waffled.

George diverted the compliments, choosing to talk about the house and let Sarah know a little more about the history, with Lady Martha agreeing at times and laughing about the amount of information George retained; finally remarking that the family had not been the same without him. *'He kept us ticking over'* she added.

Dinner was announced and they headed off to the dining room with Sarah wondering whether it would be just the three of them?

As if by reading her mind George asked whether the boys would be joining them.

'Well,' said Lady Martha with a knowing tone. *'Yes, should be the answer'* she announced *'but it appears they have busier lives these days'*

George showed Sarah to her seat, as her Ladyship was assisted by a member of staff.

'I would have loved you to meet them' George

told Sarah and Lady Martha went on to explain how Charles and Jackson adored George and that he had been softer than their father. They would often rush to George who would see how best to deal with whatever it was they were being taken to task over.

George lowered his head in agreement, his face lit with a smile.

The evening was delightful, wonderful company and wonderful food, although there were moments when Sarah wondered why she had been invited? It was apparent these two could talk about old times all they wanted but with her present, they politely kept conversation centred to the Cove, memories they could all share and the knowledge that it always brought people together and often back home.

By the end of the evening Sarah was floating ... so much to take in, so much to think about and the beauty of it all was she felt at ease, with herself mostly but also her surroundings, which was a big deal when she thought about her earlier insecurity. She had got up and gone out and look how the day had evolved.

Lady Martha had been gracious and kind and although they would never be fond friends, she knew how special it was to be in her company and George told Sarah on their drive home that he knew Lady Martha well enough to say she was relaxed and enjoyed herself. He also mentioned that he wished she had been fortunate to have a daughter, as her sons were busy doing their own thing. Sarah had to agree she was missing her Mum, more so tonight; Lady Martha with all her wealth and comfort, would never know the joy of having a daughter.

Edward drove the car so gently down the hillside and George pointed out some of the views on the horizon and helped place the layout of the town for Sarah.

Finally, they reached the top of the lane but ever the gentleman, George insisted on walking Sarah back to the beach hut.

'Look at these George' Sarah cooed as she hurriedly opened the front door and encouraged him inside. George was close behind her and with wide eyes, he started to move the photographs around, studying them carefully. Sarah turned on the main light and the two were engrossed.

Sarah held up one of her Grandmother and smiled, *'Here she is'* she beamed proudly, then noticed as his tone remained soft, fondly speaking her name.

She then pointed out the one of her Mum and her as a little girl and George gave out a little chuckle, *'Look out, there's trouble'* he said.

As they discussed the photographs, Sarah noticed he held on to one of her Grandmother a little longer and moving his glasses to the end of his nose he focused and it crossed her mind to ask if he knew her, but something held her back.

'*Too late for a cuppa*?' Sarah asked '*I don't think I could sleep just yet*' she explained as she put the kettle on. George cleared his throat, then said he would, but just a small one. '*I have to get up in the night if I drink late*' he laughed, '*it's an old age thing*'. He smiled again and replaced the photos on the table.

Sarah removed her locket and laid it down next to her Grandmother's photo '*This was hers*' she said and opened the locket to show George the small photograph of her Grandmother on one side and her Mother on the other. '*It's the only keepsake I have*' she said softly.

Sarah continued to make drinks while George pulled the open locket close, placing his glasses on the bridge of his nose and taking another look. '*Beautiful*' he agreed and gently stroked his thumb across their faces. This time Sarah took note of his gentle touch and wondered why he showed such tenderness to faces he didn't know – but then the question popped into her mind once more and she wondered whether that was so? Had they been friends, or something more?

It was late and she realised she was willing this charming man to be more than he was; a knight in shining armour. If there had been a connection, she felt certain he would have said something by now. The hour was late so a quick drink and chat would suffice.

George rose first and thanked Sarah for being his companion for the evening and Sarah put her arms around him and held him tight, thanking him for being such a good friend during her time of need and asking him to let her know if she could repay him in any way.

'I'm good' he told her, *'happy to have a friend in you'* he said and with that he wished her a good night and pulled the door behind him.

Sarah spread the photos on the table once more and holding the one of her Grandmother closer to the light she said, *'Sorry it's been so long'*. She then kissed her picture and placed it down next to her Mum and knew that she would sleep better tonight.

Chapter Six

The following morning Sarah felt rejuvenated and grateful to be alive. She leapt out of bed and hurried to the kitchen table and smiled broadly as she viewed the ladies in her life. Holding their memory was one thing, seeing them so closely brought them into her reality and made the loneliness bearable.

The sun was up, streaming through the windows so Sarah pushed the curtains aside, so it flooded the room. She closed her eyes, drew in her breath and welcomed the heat on her face.

She wondered about George and his reaction the night before and yes, she has seen too many afternoon dramas to allow her imagination to run away with her but just for one moment, wouldn't it be wonderful if he had had a relationship with her Grandmother, for their love affair to have produced a baby girl (her Mother), only for her to find her long lost Grandfather, all these years later?

Sarah brushed the hair from her eyes, she had always been told not to ask about him. Maybe he had been married? George did say he loved two women but only married one. But George, a love cheat? Guess he was young once and following recent events, she knew only too well that anything was possible.

She looked down at her toes, wriggled them in the ray of sun, then smiled to herself as she snapped out of her fantasy – poor George, best not to mention any of that, she decided.

Sarah made herself a little scrambled egg, then text Beth and asked if she was free to call later. She knew School term was nearing the end and today she felt up to talking, probably due to having had a relaxing and rewarding day yesterday. Beth said she would let her know when she was home and was looking forward to it; seeing her name appear on the screen confirmed to Sarah how much she missed her.

'*Hey, Hugo come here!*' came a shout. Sarah opened the doors at the front of the hut just as Hugo came bounding in, taking a small coffee table over with him. Sarah squealed and fell back into the armchair.

'*Hugo!*' the man shouted as he followed behind, slipping as he did and trying to regain control of his dog. Hugo, being a bulldog, had no intention of listening and ran around the furniture causing for a comical scene to unfold.

Sarah laughed as she pulled her feet up onto the seat and each time Hugo bombed past, he caught something else, taking with him a plant pot and stand, then sliding into the kitchen and into the cupboard doors with a large thud.

Eventually the man grabbed his harness and the two came to an abrupt halt, one on top of the other.

'Y*ou knob!*' he yelled, then he looked up to

see Sarah defending herself in the corner. '*Oh, shit*' he exclaimed and raising to his feet quickly, hanging on to Hugo's harness firmly as he did. '*I am so sorry!*' he said and this time he was red and embarrassed.

'*I didn't know anyone was staying here*' he looked at Sarah for reassurance, then down to his furry friend and gave him a tap with his trainer on the rump. '*You mate are in big trouble*' he berated him, but Hugo wasn't bothered at all. He was panting heavily and having a brilliant time.

'*He's a dog that likes to f… nope, can't say that!*' he corrected himself. Sarah raised herself up saying she was fine but looking around the place she was concerned about damage to George's property.

'*It's Jack, isn't it?*' she asked. Jack was picking up the plant pot and holder.

'*Well remembered … Sarah?*' he checked, but without certainty. '*I really am sorry, and I will help put it right*' Jack continued. '*Just let me tie him up on the veranda*'

Jack dragged the beast past Sarah, but she managed to stroke Hugo as he passed.

'*No permanent damage by the looks of it*' she confirmed.

They tidied up the place and Sarah offered Hugo some water which he then spread out across the veranda

'Yeah, another one of his helpful tricks' said Jack with an expression of frustration and bewilderment at his mate's continuous need to cause trouble for him.

'I know George' Jack said. *'and I will explain it's all my fault and I really am sorry for barging in like this.'* Sarah said it was fine and she would talk to George later.

'Day off?' she asked, *'Paramedic? That's* right, isn't it?'

'Yes, good memory' Jack replied, perching on the stool near the table. *'day off'* Jack sighed aloud *'Family stuff to do'*.

'Oh, that sounded ominous' Sarah giggled, and Jack raised one eyebrow, adding *'It is, trust me!'*

Jack got up to leave, firstly checking once more, all was ok and then asked her if she was enjoying her time in the Cove – apart from a Hugo invasion, and thankfully, she said she was. He also asked her if she was still planning on staying for the summer and after Sarah said *'definitely'* Jack mumbled *'That's good to know'* unaware he had spoke out loud.

Jack stepped off the veranda with Hugo in tow, then turning to Sarah he paused *'Are you up for a drink?'* he asked. *'I owe you an apology?'* Sarah shook her head, *'It's not necessary, but thank you'* she smiled.

'*Can't persuade you*?' Jack tried again but Sarah declined once more. '*No, thank you, not at the moment*'. She replied.

Jack accepted it was time to leave, then turned and walked away with Hugo dragging behind him; '*Bad boy*!' she heard him lightly scold.

By midday the heat was a little uncomfortable and it was difficult to feel the breeze even with the sea on her doorstep so she decided to change.

A strappy top and a relax for a few minutes on her bed seemed a good idea; the room offering a cooler retreat at the back of the hut. Plus, her late night had caught her up.

Fashing lights from the side of the hut drew her attention and Sarah realised it was an emergency service.

She opened the front door for a better look and standing on her tip toes, she felt her heart skip a beat; was that where George lived?

Sarah hurried through the small intertwining lanes and winding paths in her best effort to head in the right direction. George had only pointed out his place the one time and she found herself unable to decide which one it was when she had been out on a recent walk but there was no time. She was prepared to be embarrassed when she got there if she was incorrect, but luckily, she saw the flag blowing in the breeze and rushed towards it.

Upon arrival, a small handful of faces, possibly neighbours, were gathering and she knew she was at the right place when she could see George being made comfortable on a stretcher.

She squeezed past a few people, excusing herself as she made her way to the room and crouched down next to him, clasping his hand tightly. He looked up, then attempting to remove his oxygen mask she heard him mutter her name, before the mask was replaced by the Paramedic. '*No, don't talk George*' Sarah insisted and squeezed his hand gently once more.

She was new to the area so didn't know who knew who, or if any of the people in the room were George's family but as the stretcher was being lifted onto the trolley, Sarah asked which Hospital George was being taken to and said she would follow.

The lady in the corner turned around and Sarah realised it was the ice-cream mugger and nearby was her unfortunate victim. He stepped forward and asked George who Sarah was but before she had a chance to explain for herself, the lady raised her hand '*No time for that Charles*' she snapped, '*Get him a few toiletries and a change of clothes and let's go*'. *C*harles dutifully obeyed.

Sarah left abruptly and climbed the stone steps, hurriedly making her way up the lane leading to the street where she struggled to get a signal on her phone, so asked a nearby shop if they could call her a taxi.

'Nothing local' she was told, but they agreed to try for her and said it would take around 20 minutes. *'20 Minutes?'* she exclaimed, *'Where's it coming from?'*

She sighed aloud and realised the look of surprise on the shop keeper's face, *'Sorry'* she said, *'Need to get to the Hospital, I don't mean to be rude and it was kind of you to help me, please forgive me'*

The shopkeeper moaned a *'no problem'* as Sarah made her way outside. She continued to pace up and down and watched the Ambulance head off in the distance and it occurred to her that she could be losing another person, however foolish that may appear considering the little they knew about each other, but for Sarah he had come along when her need was great and now, she felt helpless.

On her way to the Hospital Sarah realised that she may not get to see George; she wasn't family and being a person renting his hut for the summer, hardly qualified as next of kin. Then there was the couple in the room who dismissed her out of hand but at least she could say she was there, and George had seen her, albeit briefly.

Inside the Hospital, confusion reigned and the smell was too familiar that Sarah struggled to focus when she arrived at the reception. Suddenly she realised she didn't know George's full name or any personal details; *'his address perhaps?* The receptionist suggested, but Sarah shook her head and tearfully whispered *'no, sorry'.*

'Hi' a voice called over Sarah's shoulder and she was so grateful to recognise a face. *'Hi'* she answered in desperation, *'Can you help me?'*

Sarah grabbed his arm and pulled him to one side, but he raised his finger in a bid to hold for one moment and then she heard him ask the receptionist to confirm where George had been taken.

Sarah gasped, *'Of course, you know George?'* then turned to the receptionist *'That's the George I was asking about'* she continued. *'I gathered that'* came the curt reply.

Jack took Sarah's hand off his arm and took her to one side, looking a little confused himself.

'How did you find out he was in Hospital?' Jack asked and Sarah explained about the Ambulance and that she made her way across. She also explained that he had been conscious when she arrived, as he'd squeezed her hand.

Jack looked relieved to hear that, just as they were joined by Charles and his lady friend, Cynthia.

'Brother' Charles spoke, and the two men briefly embraced, with a quick peck on each cheek given to Cynthia before she gave a sideways glance to Sarah.

'Brother?' thought Sarah, realising Jack is

Jackson, son of Lady Martha.

'*You were at the house!*' she stated, though it sounded more like an accusation. Jack had previously remarked that this was a small place and everyone knew each other; he wasn't wrong!

'*Yes, I saw the lights*' she said, but Cynthia had already turned her eyes away and was looking to Jack for guidance, '*Where is he?*'

Jack pointed ahead and they made their way down the corridor with Sarah following behind, but Jack was very courteous and tried to include her, as they headed for the lift.

'*It will be family only*' Cynthia told him firmly, but her eyes never strayed from his and Sarah realised the statement was meant for her. Not for one moment did she think she could go in with them, but finding out where he was, would be a start.

Once they reached the right level, Jack gestured to Sarah to wait in the family room near the main desk and promised to return to her as soon as possible, once he had news. She agreed and thanked him for being so thoughtful, but he reminded her that she had shown George a great kindness by attending and he knew that would be appreciated.

It felt an age before Jack returned and he said many reassuring things whilst trying to apologise for the time it had taken, but Sarah was just happy to hear George was stable.

'He has heart meds' he told her, *'and he's been fine for so long, so it was a shock for us all'* Jack continued. *'When he's rested, we'll have a chat, but he does remember you being there and I said you were waiting outside so he wanted me to thank you'* and with that Jack placed his hand on Sarah's shoulder and was certainly surprised when she hugged him. *'Sorry'* said Sarah as she pulled herself away, her eyes a little watery *'I'm just happy he's ok; he's been so kind to me'*

Jack was smiling, his eyes shone and his stance was strong and Sarah was aware that in a good rom-com this would be the moment where the couple would kiss, unexpected, yet not to the eager audience, so she broke her gaze and picked up her bag waffling something to Jack that even she couldn't understand and asked him to give George her best; then left.

Jack gave a little chuckle but said he would and whilst he watched her hurry to the safety of the lift Charles appeared and couldn't help notice his gaze.

'Seriously Jackson' he said, slapping his shoulder and jolting him out of his stare *'Definitely not your type!'*

George continued to improve, and the family gave him round the clock support for the next 24 hours, including a visit from Lady Martha, who had insisted.

Charles escorted his mother to George's room,

then before leaving, he suggested he would return
within the hour.

Chapter Seven

The following day Sarah made her own way to the Hospital and on seeing Charles heading for the lift, she quickly tucked herself out of sight.

Once he was out of view, she came closer to the window and although the curtain was pulled across, the door was slightly ajar. Sarah stepped back and held her breath.

Although she had witnessed Charles leave, she had not realised Lady Martha remained. Suddenly, she felt a little awkward; yet she had managed to get all the way to his room without being approached and there was no reason to believe she would get this far again, so she decided to wait a moment, then announce herself.

There was a quieter moment in the corridor, less people walking by and the lift having been called away gave way to silence. It was then that Sarah overheard a little of their conversation. It was tender and their fondnes, audible.

'You gave me a scare' Lady Martha spoke softly as George stroked her hand *'You can't get rid of me that easily'* he replied.

'What was it?' she asked *'I noticed the locket*

George'. Sarah's eyes widened and she held her breath once again, but this time she clasped tightly the locket around her neck and a puzzled expression crossed her brow.

'*My locket*?' she wondered.

'*Martha*' whispered George as he tried to sit upright, but Martha stopped him.

'*No … George … rest please*' she begged. '*It's ok, it was a long time ago*' she assured him.

'*We both loved other people George*' she said and then moved herself from the chair beside his bed, to sit carefully next to him. Sarah noticed his eyes light up as she smiled upon him.

'*When did you know*?' she asked. George was shaking his head slowly.

'*She walked into the café*' he reminded her, '*Asked for directions*' he smiled broadly and Lady Martha let out a little chuckle, '*Wow, that surely is fate*' she announced and with that Sarah fled.

As she made her way to the exit her mind was full of questions, her face was flushed and she felt a little dizzy, but now panic had spread through her body, so it was all she could do to jump in the first taxi that arrived.

She had no knowledge of her journey home, no memory of any conversation, apart from a vague recollection that the driver had been trying to chat and at the other end he asked her if she was alright. She paid the fare and run down the lane to the hut. Once inside she collapsed on the floor and started to cry *'What is happening?!!'* she wailed but nobody heard her; she was the star of yet another drama.

George *knew her*? He couldn't have orchestrated any of this? No-one knew she would be returning to the Cove? So, was he her Grandfather, after all? Was the locket from him and if so, why didn't he say something?

Another night curled up on the armchair watching the light leave the beach and welcome the moon over the water – the hours went by and Sarah was oblivious to everything around her, the beach emptying and the night air become cooler.

But a message from Beth eventually broke the silence and a request to call was turned down. Beth messaged again and said she really needed to hear her voice, so Sarah relented.

'How are you?' Beth asked and Sarah gave the longest sigh ever. *'Is that a good sigh?'* Beth giggled, then realised her friend sounded exhausted and something was wrong.

'Talk to me' she begged.

'You know I'm renting this place from George?' she began.

'Yes', said Gracie, *'Your new friend?'*

'Well,' Sarah drew another deep breath.

'*No, you didn't!*' exclaimed Beth. '*Tell me you didn't?*'

Sarah interrupted '*No, of course not!*' she snapped, taking stock of hersel. '*I think George could be my Grandfather*' she announced.

Silence fell between them before Beth repeated the words very slowly '*Your G r a n d f a t h e r?*'

'*Yes*' Sarah repeated '*He didn't say he knew me or that he recognised my locket when we met, but he does; on both accounts*' she continued and then the conversation took on real speed as she let the words pour out.

'*I didn't know, obviously, in fact I had fantasied about how lovely it would be, if he was, but that was mad, of course he wouldn't be; what were the chances?*' Beth managed to butt in, '*exactly ... Sarah can you hear yourself?*'

'*I know how it sounds*' she continued, '*he took me to dinner and I met Lady Martha ...*'

'*Lady Martha?*' quoted Beth but was immediately shut down by Sarah's venting.

'*Yes, a friend of George's, he was in service and he was rushed to Hospital yesterday and I overheard Lady Martha ask him about the locket; my locket!*'

It was Beth's turn to sigh deeply, then she tried another approach, '*darling, you have been through so much, probably not a lot makes sense right now. You should have stayed with me, you're grieving Sarah*'

Sarah started to cry and Beth tried desperately to comfort her from afar *'Come home'* she pleaded. *'Let me look after you, please come home. I'm worried about you'*

Sniffling, Sarah pulled the throw up to her chin and wiped her nose.

> *'I've been so happy here Beth, I just don't know what the connection is and I'm tired, that's all, just tired. Don't worry, please?'*

The two promised to talk in the next couple of days and Sarah promised Beth that she would make it to bed and that was something she felt she could manage. Her body ached and her head was pounding from crying, her eyes puffy and tender so the deep eiderdown was a welcome comfort and thankfully sleep came quickly.

Chapter Eight

During the night Sarah woke a few times, turning over and over and re-thinking last night's events. Then she went further back and tried to put together memories where she had asked her Mother about her Grandad and had been told that he died – for years that was acceptable as a child, but when she was older, in her late teens and talking with her Mum about the possibility of moving back to the Cove, she had asked again and had been told not to keep questioning. It was private, they had a love affair, resulting in her Mum being born and finally, that he was an older man and not free to marry.

Sarah remembers thinking he must have been

married but another conversation ruled that out and she was told to accept it. Her Grandmother had always said she knew they could never marry and even when she found out she was pregnant, she accepted she would be having the baby alone and this caused a lot of controversy at the time and her parents were ostracised.

Due to the sensitive nature and cloud that shrouded their story, Sarah had to let it go. Now she wondered whether her Mum had ever found out who her father was, or did she accept her mother's wishes and let it lie.

She had always wanted to return to the Cove and would she have done that if she knew he was still there? She had never mentioned the name George, not that Sarah could recall?

Sarah rose, there was no point in lying there any longer so she dressed and decided that she would ask George when he was well enough. It was her life and if there was something he knew; she had the right to know it too. How could she make a new life in the Cove, surrounded by more secrets?

The sun was hiding that morning and it looked a little darker, so Sarah picked up her jacket and gathered up a water bottle and a banana, before heading for the door. As she turned into the lane, she noticed Jack heading down, he smiled and waved.

 '*George, ok*?' Sarah was quick to ask.

Jack nodded *'Yes, great improvement'* he assured her. *'That's why I'm here actually'* Sarah held her jacket over her arm and Jack noticed she was heading off somewhere.

'Sorry it's early. I just wanted to say the Doctor has asked for no visitors today and I wanted to let you know' Sarah's eyes widened *'Why?'* she asked, as her thoughts turned to her unanswered questions.

Jack went on to explain George was having a new stent put in and would need to rest, but it was positive and knowing George the way he did, he would never tell them to stay away so the Doctor made a judgement call.

'Were you heading there?' Jack asked and pointed to her jacket.

'No, not yet' she said, *'bad night, just needed to clear my head, though I reckon we have some rain on the way'* Sarah looked to the sky and Jack agreed, saying that was the downside to living by the sea, that the weather could change from morning to afternoon, then back again with alarming speed.

'Fancy that drink?' he said, this time smiling and adding coffee would be fine, breakfast if she hadn't already eaten. Sarah returned an exhausted smile and couldn't deny that in the back of her mind she wondered if he could shed any light on George; fill in a few gaps perhaps? *'Sounds good'* she accepted, as they headed off together.

They settled down by the cafe window and whilst

Jack ordered coffee and scrambled eggs, Sarah studied him from behind. He must be around her age, maybe younger, but he was certainly in good order, she mused. He was quite toned and maybe with the demands of his job he needed to be; strong in both mind and body.

She turned her eyes away as he headed back to the table and placed a few items in front of her. '*Thank you*' she said, as Jack sat and helped the waitress who was following him, lay out their breakfast.

'*Wow, how many are we feeding*?' Sarah giggled.

'*I love breakfast*' Jack quipped, his smile broadening as he gave a little wink. '*She's eating for two*' he told the waitress, who for a moment looked surprised, then tapped him sharply on the shoulder '*Jack!*' she said. '*Always the joker*'

Sarah laughed, then thanked him for letting the girl think she was pregnant – '*Must get back to the gym*' she said. Jack gasped and bit his lip, then quickly tried to withdraw the comment.

'*No ... believe me, you've no need*' he said. '*I know her Father*' he continued and then he looked over at the young waitress who was relaying the tease to a colleague.

They started eating and a little light conversation between the two flowed. Sarah couldn't help telling Jack about his brother Charles and the two shared a when she detailed the ice-cream encounter.

'*Cynthia can't help herself*' he told her. '*Charles is obsessed with her and has asked her to marry him twice, but he is a good deal older and too stuffy she reckons*' Jack looked a little frustrated as he continued.

'*Shame really as our families grew up together and they earmarked Cynthia and Charles as the perfect pair to run the family estate, plus it's in his veins, so thankfully the right brother will be the next Lord of the Manor, so to speak*' Sarah found herself lost in the history and listened intently as he explained his father had been such a difficult man to get close to '*well … that was never going to happen*' he stated.

'*That's where George stepped in*' offered Sarah and Jack smiled, a little confused as to how she knew that, but Sarah explained how she had been to his ancestral home, had dinner with his Mother and heard how George had been a wonderful influence on the boys growing up. Then Sarah noticed the love for George show on Jack's face, '*He's a legend*' he agreed. '*When my Father died, we were taken to see Mother in the drawing room, strange really, and when she had finished explaining, we were taken to the playroom and I remember asking Charles if George would be our Father now*' His smile changed to one of thought, '*Whereas if something had happened to George, I would have been gutted.*'

Sarah knew their bond was strong and she told

Jack that she understood and that George talked about him with the same fondness.

'*Have you ever been married?*' she asked Jack to which he chortled and denied emphatically, '*Err, no thanks*' he said, then without hesitation, added '*Cynthia would have me up the aisle if she could, so I have to stand firm until Charles has worn her down*'

'*Oh really?*' Sarah replied, '*she's waiting for you?*'

'*Yes, sadly for Charles*' he explained. '*We're closer in age, but I do not want to be part of the establishment, that's not in my blood, not like it is for Charles so I told her if she wants to be the Lady the Manor, she needs to accept his proposal before he finds her replacement*'

Sarah frowned and Jack asked her what she was thinking.

'*I overheard Cynthia in the jewellery store saying he hadn't proposed yet, but he would soon, so I'm not sure who is dragging their heels?*' Jack grinned. '*I think she meant me*' he said, '*... and again, never going to happen!*' Sarah drew her breath and mumbled '*oh dear*' before they both giggled and moved on to another topic.

A few more coffees and Sarah found herself telling another stranger that she had recently buried her partner, found out about his cheating and left it all behind to return to a place she knew, a long time ago.

Jack looked surprised and she noticed a little relieved perhaps that she was free to make choices about her future; again, saying that he was glad she had returned.

It was closer to lunchtime by the time the two left and as they started to walk through the town Sarah felt so comfortable chatting to Jack, she found herself asking about George's history and if Jack had known his wife which he had. He went on to tell her that everyone was fond of her, she worked in the kitchen and was kind to them, like George.

She used to send biscuits to the boys, always found them a sweet treat when they appeared in the kitchen and had been known to hide them out the back when Nanny was searching for them.

'Sadly, they had no children' he added, *'but he had his hands quite full with us I reckon'*. Jack took Sarah's hand as they stepped over a small stone wall and walked along to a bench on the sea front. The sky looked menacing and the clouds were darkening; the air now filled with the threat of rain. *'We may have to make a run for it'* he suggested.

Suddenly a rumble overhead interrupted their conversation and Sarah looked up at the sky. *'You may be right'* she answered so they decided to make a move.

'It's quicker along the beach' Jack decided and

helped her down a couple of steps to the beach. The breeze picked up and Sarah pulled her jacket around her shoulders, feeling the first spots of rain and seeing the heavier drops leave indentations in the sand.

'It's coming' she giggled *'We're going to get soaked'*

They picked up the pace but their feet laid heavy in the sand, Jack apologised saying that perhaps they would have had a little more shelter if they had nipped down the lane but now it was too late; the heavens opened.

Sarah squealed as the rain fell hard, drenching them and within minutes their feet were caked in wet sand, rubbing between their toes. Their clothes were sticking to their skin and now Sarah's wet hair was hanging down in front of her face and with every word her mouth filled with water. Jack was trying to pull her jacket above her head as well as shelter her shoulders but trying to walk quickly with sandy boot shaped feet, they could do no more than laugh as they finally reached the veranda.

The rain bounced off the wooden deck. Jack's shirt was clinging to his torso and Sarah's dress stuck to her thighs and outlined the shape of her waist and legs.

'Let me get towels' Jack said but Sarah looked down at their feet and decided they were way be-

yond a towel, so invited Jack in until the weather eased.

Returning from the bathroom, Sarah held a white towel aound her body, just long enough to cover the important bits but short enough to show her shapely legs. She pulled the bottom together as she passed him a dressing gown.

'*Must belong to George*' she said. '*It was in the wardrobe*'.

Jack accepted the robe and headed to the bathroom, asking if he could take a quick shower to wash off the sand and Sarah agreed, suggesting she would take the next.

When he emerged, he had the robe in his arms and a towel smaller than hers wrapped around his waist; his toned stomach on show. Sarah tried to overt her eyes, but he knew exactly the reaction he was looking for and when he passed her the dressing gown, he said he wasn't a '*robe type of guy*', Sarah couldn't help but joke that she could see why.

She headed off to the shower herself and whilst rinsing Jack called to her that he would put the kettle on, if that was alright.

Eventually Sarah returned from the shower; their wet clothes hanging over the bath.

Jack suggested he could ask for something to be sent over but Sarah was quick to remind him about the little town where everyone knew everyone's business. He beamed.

'I've loved today, all things considered' he spoke softly and whilst doing so he leaned in a little, so their shoulders touched, pointing to the stormy skies.

Sarah continued to keep her eyes forward, her cup to her lips as she murmured in agreement, *'me too'* she smiled.

'Do you want to go out for dinner?' Jack tried his luck once more, aware that today had been a revelation but it could be too soon, so he tried to back track a little when the question was out but Sarah surprised herself and accepted.

'Take out sounds better?' she smiled and with that Jack placed down his cup and took hers from her hand and turned towards her.

He raised her chin and whilst holding that position for a moment, he looked into her eyes, then brushed her hair from her face with the other hand. Sarah lowered her eyes slowly, but he asked her to look at him and she did.

'You're beautiful' he told her, then slowly lowered his head and placed a tender kiss on her lips.

It felt wonderful to have the warmth of another's mouth, to feel his lips strong, yet gentle, pressing against hers. His skin was warm, yet still a little damp from the shower and Jack pulled her in close and kissed her longer, fully on the mouth until their kiss became stronger and passionate.

Sarah heard her own breathing hasten and Jack's breath was heavy around her neck as he kissed around her shoulders, his hands pulling her even closer and following the line of her back; slightly tugging the towel that covered her.

He returned to kiss her mouth again and this time there was no question they both were in need as they made their way to the bedroom, Jack pushing the door closed with his foot, behind them.

On the bed he took control and Sarah's towel was removed, sliding it from under her so carefully whilst his eyes devoured her. Her skin glistened from the shower and the hairs on her arms rose a little from the cool air, her nipples now erect from the chill and excitement of what was to come.

Jack pulled off his towel and Sarah noticed his excitement matched hers, his amazing body on show and even the realisation that she had only known Steve intimately, did not dampen her desire.

He kissed her quivering stomach and made his way up her body, her arms eagerly pulling him towards her and waiting for his mouth to search out her breasts. Jack's mouth took the opportunity of tasting every part of her body, exploring her senses and the two of them spent an afternoon of indulgence, neither wanting it to end.

Early evening was upon them before they realised,

and Jack ordered a food delivery which went back to the bedroom.

'*What are your plans for tomorrow*?' Jack asked cheekily, so happy with his conquest and his suddenly sheepish captive said she was free.

'*I do want to see George though*' she added, and Jack said they could go together, which pleased her even more.

His clothes were tumbled dry, having allowed surplus water to drip away during their adventurous afternoon.

A farewell kiss at the doorway nearly took them back to their hideaway but Sarah pushed him out and told him she needed to rest; Jack smiled, then paused for a moment, telling her that he couldn't remember when he last felt this happy. Sarah felt the same.

There's no sleep like a satisfied sleep and her body ached in a way it never had before, every part of her skin felt taken over, his touch still evident by her senses and drawing up the top sheet so that it caressed her over-sensitive body reminded her of his lips. She smiled, then giggled to herself as she drifted off to a satisfied sleep.

Chapter Nine

S arah was out of bed and excited for the first time in years – the warmth of the shower felt wonderful against her slightly bruised skin this morning. He was strong and his firm grip had left its mark, but she wasn't complaining.

The weather was dry which was a blessing, but not the sunniest so she pulled on her ¾ jeans and a tee-shirt and picked up a cardi whilst waiting for Jack. A quick bite of breakfast was eaten just as he arrived and the two embraced each other good morning.

'*We have time*' he winked but Sarah declined.

'*Let's go*' he laughed.

Jack told her that he had called the Hospital first thing and George was resting, all had gone well with the procedure and he had been asked to call back after lunch to see whether visitors were allowed.

He talked her into a little road trip, '*not far*' he promised, but just enough to get a feel of the place and again, this was something Sarah was happy to accept and it wasn't long before she recognised a restaurant where her Mum had been a waitress, so Jack promised to take her for lunch on the way back.

It so surprised Sarah just how at ease she was with him. They were driving around with Jack regailing stories about his family's involvement in the town, how his Grandfather before him had helped with a re-build and the locals had come together in thanks, keeping their homes and land safe and strong, against the elements.

He talked with pride and she knew that his relationship with his Father was a little cooler than he would have liked but she could see how that was possible when his Mother had been a young woman from a wealthy family, encouraged to marry his Father who was 15 years older. It wasn't love he told Sarah, but his Mother said she was very fond of him. She hadn't known any other man and when she was 18, she married and Charles came along 9 months later but for years she thought he would be an only child as her husband found it difficult to be affectionate.

One-time Lady Martha had asked her Father if she could return home but her Mother had been sent to stay with her for a weekend and by the time she left, Lady Martha had been convinced things would improve.

'Quite lonely' Jack noted *'Wouldn't happen these days'* he added *'I don't think he was capable of showing love'*

Sarah noted the time as they made their way back towards the town and stopped at the restaurant where her Mum had worked. She smiled as they entered the building and when the waiter asked if they wanted a table Sarah found herself sharing her history.

Lunch ordered and a glass of wine brought over, Sarah told Jack she never thought she would have found herself on a date only a few days after burying her partner? She then frowned and sat back, *'Wow, what does that say about me?'* she added, but Jack reached for her hand.

'Don't do that' he said calmly, *'you have been on the wrong side of happiness for a some time, from the sounds of it. Please don't regret this'* Sarah smiled, her eyes a little watery, but she smiled wider as he finished his statement. *'I don't'* she confirmed.

After lunch they made their way to the Hospital and George had been given the all clear for visitors. They giggled like a pair of lovebirds in the lift and could not keep their hands off each other, kissing, then breaking free when the doors opened.

As they arrived, Jack opened the door for Sarah and George's face beamed; and Sarah was surprised to see him sitting upright, bright and alert.

'You look so well' she noted.

'Good to see you too' George said and told her he remembered her at the house, saying it was kind of her to come and check on him.

'You didn't know what you were getting your-self into, when you took on the hut, did you?' he grinned.

'Happy to' Sarah insisted and sat herself carefully on the edge of the bed.

Jack followed her in and shook George's hand, tell-ing him to stop the late-night boozing which at first caught Sarah off guard, then she realised he was teasing.

'*Always the joker*' George explained, '*... always has been*'.

'*Well,*' said Sarah, '*Jackson should know better; the patient is supposed to be resting*' and with that Jack placed his hands on her shoulders whilst standing behind her; causing Sarah giggle.

George watched as the two flirted with each other, then he asked Sarah if she would kindly ask at the Nurse's station for some fresh water.

'*I'll get it for you now*' she offered and quickly rose, collecting his empty jug as she left the room, Jack giving her the warmest smile.

George tapped the bed and Jack sat down. '*What's going on*?' he asked but this time his expression was one of concern, confusion even. Jack by return looked puzzled and tapped the old man's hand.

'*It's all good*' he assured him. '*Sarah told me about her partner, what she's been through, we're just having fun*'

George tried to cough and Jack stood up to assist him, adjusting his pillows and keeping pressure on his back while he tried to clear the phlegm.

He was still trying to get his breath back when Charles and Cynthia arrived; the largest bunch of flowers in front of her face entering first.

'*George*' she cooed. '*You gave us a scare*'

and with that Cynthia air kissed George on both cheeks, followed by Charles who shook his hand.

As Sarah returned to the room, she saw Cynthia trying to kiss Jack on the cheek, but he withdrew, which Cynthia took notable offence to. '*Not feeling it today, Jackson*?' she quipped.

Jack didn't respond but held out his hand and took the jug of water from Sarah who felt very awkward indeed. Cynthia glanced at Sarah, then back at Jack and made a strange snorting sound of disapproval and said quietly that she was surprised he had forgotten his position.

Jackson took that as time to leave and saying farewell to George, he gestured to Sarah that they would come back tomorrow and let him rest today. George was uncharacteristically quiet, and Jack looked back, asking him if he was ok and of course, with such an audience, he convinced them he was.

Heading back to the lift Jack apologised to Sarah but she said it wasn't something that bothered her, but she certainly didn't want to cause him a problem.

'*Trust me, I live my own life*' he said, in such a way that it was not open for discussion.

Jack reached for Sarah's hand as they walked through the Hospital car park and she smiled to herself as she took hold. It was so strange to be walking hand in hand with a man she only met days ago and then a thought crossed her mind and her stomach turned over as if she had been caught out. Imagine if Beth showed up, or worse, Jean?

'*You, ok?*' asked Jack, as he opened the car door. Sarah snapped out of her trance and quickly replied she was, but Jack knew she was mulling something over so again he apologised for Cynthia's rudeness and Sarah wasn't sure he believed her when she said that it wasn't on her mind.

Their journey was quiet, unlike their trip to the Hospital when they were flirty young lovers who had just spent the afternoon in bed together.

Sarah pointed to the bus stop near the top of the lane and asked Jack to pull over, he looked a little surprised.

'*No invite?*' he asked. '*It's been an amazing day and I cannot thank you enough for making me feel so wanted*' she started. Jack looked wounded but kept quiet while she explained.

'*I promise you; this has nothing to do with Cynthia, or anyone else for that matter*' she continued and touched his knee as she softly explained that she needed to process so much, she still needed to take time out for herself and she hoped he could let her take things slow, and of course, he agreed.

Jack kissed the back of her hand. '*As long as you are ok*' he repeated.

They said their goodbyes and Sarah made her way down the lane and although earlier that afternoon she was sure she wanted to have him with her tonight, the thought that had unnerved her in the car park, now plagued her.

Then she over analysed, something Beth said she did to the point of destruction and perhaps that was true? She questioned every aspect of their relationship, albeit brief, it felt real, heady and carefree and full of passion yes, but she didn't know him and this could be more like a brief affair and that's what it felt like when she thought of Beth and Jean. She could be caught at any moment, so it was very clear that she had not yet drawn a line between her old life and the new.

When she thought of Steve, there was disappointment and resentment. That wasn't a love she needed to protect; it was toxic.

Thinking of Jack, she felt butterflies and remembered their afternoon together. It was amazing and she had never felt like that with Steve, ever! Just the thought of Jack's touch caused her skin to tingle but then her conscience got to her and she pushed thoughts of Jack to the back of her mind.

A long soak in the bath felt like the right thing to do and pouring herself a glass of wine, Sarah let the bubbles soak her skin. The sound of the sea was still audible even with the doors and windows closed and with just a few candles around for light, she was relaxed and happy to be in her own company for a while.

That night Sarah lay in bed trying to make sense of recent events but to no avail. She grabbed her pillow and putting it over her face she screamed into it, then launched it across the room.

She sighed and remembered George, laying in Hospital, hoping to be discharged tomorrow and thought how lucky she was; her new life ahead of her, then another sigh of relief.

Chapter Ten

Sarah woke the next morning with a message from Beth and it confirmed the date of the Will reading. She messaged back saying she would return to collect her belongings and would stay with Beth, accepting her kind offer. The two had a lot to catch up on and she pictured Beth's expression when she mentioned 'handsome Jack'!

Lady Martha put down the receiver and slowly

walked away from her desk, to stand in front of the large bay window at the back of the drawing room. She drew a deep breath and then used a small white handkerchief to stifle a discreet cry.

Over the years she had accepted that she may not be the only woman her husband shared a bed with. In fact, her own Father had numerous relationships and there was an understanding that her Mother told her would require her to look the other way.

She had questioned this on occasion and when trying to speak to her husband, she had been shut down, the conversation not entertained. He used to deny any such liaisons but in the same breath refused to explain his absence.

Their age gap played a part for sure, but for him, it was the frustration that she appeared so needy. He hoped that when Charles came along, she would feel her duty as a Mother, enough to warrant some time apart and he used to extend his travels saying it was best for Charles to have routine, so Martha would be expected to stay behind.

That said, when he was home, he used to scold her for spending too much time playing with Charles, when there was a perfectly suitable Nanny in the house. It led to a lonely existence for her and finally she gave in and endured many luncheons solely for the purpose of company.

Her telephone conversation with George was twofold; to say he was being discharged and then to let her know that Jack was fond of Sarah and Lady Martha could no longer deny her existence.

There had been rumours, many rumours over the years but as previously stated, always denied and nothing came of them.

Martha knew this one to be true. She had allowed George to bring his new companion to sit at her table, share memories with her and noticed the locket.

Before getting married Martha had been informed about Ellie, who her husband truly loved, but like her, his family expected better of him and he could not marry beneath him. There had been strong words from his Father and he knew he would be cut off if he disobeyed and although he could have dealt with that, there was the threat that Ellie would be named and it would bring great shame on her and her family and that was the leverage they needed. Sadly, he had to end their relationship, unaware that she was pregnant. A grand wedding took place and the town celebrated as the new Lord and Lady started their lives together.

Ellie refused to say who the Father was, but word eventually made its way back to his Lordship and there was talk of him having a breakdown, something the household covered up.

George played his part and on occasions took gifts to Ellie for the baby, he had also been turned away when he tried to offer monetary gifts, or help to ease her daily struggle.

Sarah's Grandmother had always been an independent woman and the stories she heard whilst growing up described her Grandmother as someone admired deeply. Her own Mother saying she had mellowed over the years; luckily Sarah knew her softer side.

His Lordship had commissioned the locket as a gift to Ellie for her 30th birthday and George had collected it from the designer himself and delivered it personally. Initially Ellie had refused the gift, reminding George that he was married, that it was inappropriate for her to accept it, but eventually George managed to persuade her to accept this parting gift, sent with love and respect. He also promised he would do his best to make it clear that this would be the last thing.

When Ellie opened the locket, she was touched to see it had a photograph of her and their daughter inside, and an inscription devoting his undying love to them both.

He wrote a small card that told Ellie he wished he had been a better man, choosing her and leaving his privileged life behind and Ellie found strength in his words; choosing to continue her life alone.

So that was that, nobody would ever know apart from George but unfortunately, the locket had been found by Lady Martha, prior to it being gifted to Ellie. It didn't have a photograph in it at the time but whilst her husband was away she questioned George, hoping she hadn't spoilt the surprise, presuming it was a gift for her.

George had been so fond of Lady Martha and could not understand his Lordship's indifference. She was beautiful and kind, so patient and nurturing; he felt so torn with his hidden affection and that of his loyalty to her husband.

Charles was a small boy and kept them both busy when his Lordship was away, and it was on this day that George was presented with the box containing the locket.

It had both his Lordship's initial and an 'E' entwined on the front and an inscription on the back. At the time Lady Martha questioned George, she thought the words were for her and Charles, not realising her mistake.

When his Lordship returned and Christmas came and went, Lady Martha took George to one side and asked him about the gift. He knew the day would come and hadn't dared to mention to his Lordship for fear of being dismissed himself, but by now he and Martha had become quite close.

She made it easy for him and started by saying she knew she wasn't the only one and even though George tried to offer support and reassurance, she smiled sweetly and asked him if it was over; that at least, George was able to confirm.

Jack arrived at the house and taking a few steps at a time, entered the main hallway with a hearty *'hello'*. Lady Martha was waiting in the sitting room and held out her arms to her son.

'Hello Mother' Jack beamed and held her close for a moment. *'How are you?'* he asked, before they sat down for tea.

Jack knew something was troubling her and the moment they were alone in the room and the door had closed, the silence was deafening.

'Good news about George' Martha finally remarked, but Jack knew there was more.

'I know and he should be discharged later today' Jack replied, waiting for the next instalment.

'Edward picking him up?' His mother confirmed, then stood and steadied herself at the mantlepiece.

Jack looked up, *'what's troubling you?'* he asked, his voice warm and inviting. Lady Martha turned around and Jack could see the emotion in her face and a little tear in her eye, something he was not used to seeing. He rose quickly and held her hand, *'Tell me?'* he implored.

'I need you to stop seeing Sarah' she whispered and with that Jack withdrew his hand.

'Please, just trust me' she tried to mutter, but her voice warbled, and she had to cough to clear

her throat. *'No good can come of it'* she managed to add.

Jack stepped back and stared at her with dismay, again asking her to tell him what she had against Sarah; was this about marriage?

'Jackson, please' she begged, as yet another tear appeared. *'I'm asking you to do this, for me?'*

Jack sat down and put his head in his hands and this encouraged Lady Martha to join him, this time close enough to hold his arm.

He looked to her for explanation, something that would make sense but then with a sharp tone he explained that he cared for Sarah, and that he would not be marrying Cynthia or anyone else she may have in mind. Charles was the one she should focus on; he had a life and career of his own, thank you very much!

'No, no' Martha cried, *'It's not Cynthia, or marriage for the sake of the family, I would never ask that from either of you!'*

'Mother' Jack stood up and assisted her to her feet. *'Tell me what this is about, or I'm leaving'* he demanded.

Lady Martha started to pace, concentrating on her breathing and trying to explain as best she could that the girl her son cared for could be the grand-daughter of his Father?

Jack shook his head in disbelief, then words escaped his mouth that shocked her.

'It's true Jackson, I wish it wasn't, but it really is' She continued, 'Your Father had loved another and was forced to give her up, to marry me' She looked across for recognition from her son, but he was still shaking his head in denial. 'I believe they loved each other very much, and a baby girl was born'

Jack paced the room, back and forth, back and forth, trying desperately not to hear the words, but never had his Mother lied to him before.

Lady Martha wiped her eyes, pleading with Jack to let her finish, but he was unable to.

He was having difficulty breathing and felt light-headed, so finally agreed to sit at the desk by the window, his Mother passed him some water.

'So ... Sarah? ... the lady I took to bed yesterday, is in fact, my niece?' He stared at his Mother who in turn gasped, then looked like she fell into a trance. 'My niece?' Jack continued, only this time with volume. 'Fuck!'

Lady Martha felt giddy herself, so it was Jack's turn to assist her. He walked away from her, towards the window, then returned and held his chest.

'Mother, could you be mistaken?' he begged, with every part of his being, now crouching beside her and clasping her hand in a desperate bid for the story to be retracted.

'I recognised her locket' she said so quietly

that it was hardly audible. Shock had set in and all she could think now was that she was too late; her son had crossed a line and life had repeated itself. The house would have another secret to hold.

'*Your Father had the locket made for her Grandmother, for her birthday*' she continued. Jack stood up abruptly, his fingers constantly pushing his hair from his face, sweat appearing on his brow.

'*The locket could have been bought from a charity shop*' Jack suggested in desperation '*that cannot be the evidence you're basing my future on?*'

Lady Martha snapped out of her stare and raised her voice, '*Jackson*' she barked. '*George noticed it, he was the one who helped with the design all those years ago and delivered it himself to Sarah's Grandmother ... '*. She took a breath and continued. '*The locket holds a picture of Sarah's Grandmother and Sarah's Mother inside; she showed it to us at dinner*'

Jack walked over to the fireplace and his Mother followed him, this time placing her clammy hand on his shoulder. '*I wish it wasn't so*' she whispered quietly.

He studied her expression and for a moment thought about his Mother's predicament. Living in a loveless marriage, having to endure his Father's temperament, knowing he wished he could be somewhere else.

Jack kissed her cheek and said he would do the

right thing, but she needed to give him time. He asked her not to say anything to Charles and they both agreed to keep it between themselves for now, as Jack knew he would need to talk with George before he spoke to Sarah, in the vague hope that his Mother was mistaken.

Chapter Eleven

The morning arrived for Sarah to return home and the restless night before was a reminder that she hadn't conquered as many hurdles as she first thought. Her escape was necessary and this new chapter of her life had given hope and happiness that she could not have imagined.

Now though, she was boarding a bus, wary of the welcome that lay ahead and unsure she was strong enough to deal with sorrowful faces and apologies from so-called friends.

Unfortunately, there was no avoiding it, today had to be faced and thinking of Jack, Sarah smiled to herself; just knowing someone cared for her, truly lifted her spirits.

The bus left the Cove on time and as the coast road opened out ahead of them, Sarah knew one thing for sure … she was coming back!

The return train journey gave plenty of time for thought and she took the opportunity of talking with Beth. They arranged a pickup from the Station and Sarah couldn't help but giggle when Beth said she sounded happier, but she decided she would keep her waiting just a little longer. She wanted to see her face when she mentioned Jack.

She also realised she had to see Jean, collect her things and go to the hearing, yet all Sarah wanted to do was jump forward in time and be on the train journey back, leaving her past well and truly behind.

She sat back and rested her tired head and closed her eyes, as the sun beamed through the windows and warmed her face.

Surprisingly Jack had been quiet … worryingly so. Hope he hadn't changed his mind about her now they had slept together? She sat up and checked her phone again. The last message he sent was that he was sorry he couldn't get to see her before she left and he hoped all would be well, telling her he would see her soon. There wasn't anything cold about it, but then it wasn't quite as previous texts. Sarah shook her head and snapped herself out of it.

Recent weeks, pain and misunderstanding had caused her to feel quite anxious when there wasn't anything to worry about and she knew she had to manage that better.

Finally, the train pulled into the Station and the bustling began. Sarah stepped back for a moment and let those in a hurry rush by, choosing to take stock of herself, control her unsettled stomach and breathe a little slower.

Thankfully Beth's squeals were easy to hear as she pushed her way through the sea of faces and fell into a tight embrace with Sarah laughing, then crying, holding tight.

'I've missed you SOOO much' squealed Beth, then pulling back she placed her hands on her shoulders.

'Don't cry' she cooed. *'You're ok Sarah. We'll do this together'* Sarah only managed a gentle nod as they continued to hug.

Beth picked up the holdall and Sarah a smaller bag as they walked away together, linked by arms, smiling at each other and both trying to speak over the noise until they arrived at the taxi rank.

The journey back was a little quieter with Sarah lost in thought, aware that Beth was still talking, her volume muted. Then Beth touched Sarah's leg and it brought her back to the conversation.

'*Let's go to mine first*' she said reassuringly. Sarah gave her a smile; she was so kind.

Sarah nodded in agreement and managed to reply, '*that would be good*'.

The morning unfolded and a call to Jean, although laboured, was made and they would head there later that afternoon.

Jean had managed to empty the flat of Steve's belongings and had given Sarah the opportunity of looking through them in case she wanted anything, but Sarah cut the sentence short. She had also managed to give notice on the tenancy, taking the death certificate along and settled the rent which Sarah offered to pay back, but Jean declined, again apologising for the upset caused to her.

It was agreed that tomorrow they would pop to the flat and collect her things, but Sarah could not wait to pull that door behind her.

She already knew she would not be returning – that felt right, so at some point she would have to contact School and let them know.

Having spent her working life there, she was surprised how easy a decision it was, considering the finality of it.

Beth lowered her face and made a sad expression, before smiling and saying she understood; then joked that she may be moving to join Sarah if the sea air could help her skin glow in the same way.

The hearing was tomorrow morning and that was a strange one. Sarah had never attended a Will reading before and awhile ago it was a frightening prospect, knowing she had just buried her life partner and every day after that was about her being alone, stepping in a direction she was unfamiliar with, convincing herself to take it one day at a time but now … now she just wanted it over, to get back on the train and leave it all behind her. In fact, she was questioning whether she had to attend at all?

Thankfully, Beth was the voice of reason and advised Sarah that if she didn't care then why was it a problem to see it through? *'Why leave loose ends?'*, she had stated. True enough, she needed to know there was nothing left unsaid so whatever came her way, she had to deal with it head on, then she could walk away with a clear conscience.

Beth arrived with a huge mug of tea and a few biscuits.

'Here you go' she beamed *'I've missed you so much'* she said again, and this time Sarah found her strength *'Me too'.*

'So, tell me, what's been going on?' Beth asked, pulling her feet up beneath her on the chair. Sarah

started to laugh, and it felt really good.

'You won't believe me' she teased.

'Come on, tell me' Beth begged. *'Are you still at the beach hut?'*

'Yes', said Sarah, a little smug, then placing down her steaming mug, she added. *'Still there and I can stay for the summer but George, the man I'm renting from, was rushed to hospital'*

Sarah continued, *'He's ok now. In fact, he's due home today. I saw him in Hospital ... oh he's lovely Beth, really lovely. I don't know what I would have done if I hadn't met him. Honestly, meeting him was like fate offering me a hand.'*

They spent the next hour or so chatting and Beth had been trying to fill in the gaps. She knew Sarah was renting a beach property, that a friendly face had come to her aid and she also knew that she had been excited when finding photographs of her Grandmother's shop, especially those of her Mum and so many small, much needed steps towards a happier life, but Jack was a surprise.

Beth's jaw dropped, then her eyes widened, and she clasped her hand over her mouth. *'Go You!'* she squealed with delight and again the two laughed.

'ooh, go on ... was it good?' her eyebrows raised and her eyes desperately searching Sarah's for detail. Sarah picked up her tea, sipped, then beamed the best smile Beth had seen in a long

time. *'The best!'* she chuckled.

Beth was a willing recipient and soaked up every minute detail Sarah divulged, even more taken aback by Jack's background, his family history and large estate. *'Wow'* Beth replied, sitting back and looking every bit shell shocked *'Downton Abbey!'* she oozed.

'Not quite,' laughed Sarah. *'In fact, he's just a down to earth guy and don't forget I met him as a Paramedic; he's not a stuffy type, honestly'* Sarah stopped for a moment, drank more tea, then a little more serious an expression took over and she looked over at Beth who was still drinking in the ambience of the fairy-tale.

'Have you heard from Dan? She asked. Beth snapped out of her stare, *'Not really'* she said and explained how the few times she had seen him, he had been passing by, only one of those times had he tried to stop and talk but Beth found it difficult. Also, at the time Lois had been with him and she knew it. She had tugged Dan's arm a couple of times saying that she wished Sarah well and hoped to see her when she came for the reading, but Dan was keen to talk – *'just couldn't listen to him'* Beth explained.

'Will you come with me this afternoon?' Sarah asked.

'Yes, of course' Beth agreed. *'I will drive you wherever you need to go, you are not alone Sarah'*

'*Seriously, thank you*' came Sarah's grateful reply as she reached over and placed her hand on Beth's.

'*Shall we get it over with*?' Sarah decided but Beth glanced at the clock, '*it's really early?*' she pointed out '*We arranged late afternoon?*' but Sarah said she couldn't bear the wait so the two prepared themselves to leave.

Arriving outside Jean's house, Sarah took a deep breath and Beth reminded her they could leave at any time. Sarah agreed and the two strode up the path together.

As they knocked on the door Beth reminded Sarah she held a key, but it didn't feel right in the circumstances. Sarah intended to leave the key behind this time and taking it out of her bag, she knocked again.

As she did the neighbour appeared, a very good friend to Jean over the years. '*Sarah love*' she said. Sarah and Beth were taken by surprise and Sarah blushed as she turned to answer. '*Hi Julie*'

Julie was of a similar age to Jean and she walked a little closer to the fence, then acknowledged Beth and reached her hand out to Sarah, who took it, without thinking.

She clasped her hand inside hers and offered her support and assurance that things may look bleak at the moment, but they would improve.

Sarah withdrew her hand and thanked her, but it made her realise she was back to the sympathetic eyes, the slightly undermining tone, wrapped in words of comfort.

'*Did Jean know you were coming*?' she asked.

Sarah was peering through the side window. '*Well, I am early. We spoke this morning and I said I would be round late afternoon, so maybe she's out*'

Julie nodded and muttered something the friends could not quite understand, then stepped back and raised her hand, '*Yes, ... she'll be back soon, i'm sure. You have a key, don't you*?' Julie suggested and when Sarah nodded, she said it was good to see her, and made her way in doors. Beth looked at Sarah '*Odd?*' she commented.

Sarah turned the key and entered the house.

The smell was familiar, strangely comforting, yet not homely any longer. The room was dark but no voices filled the hallway or living room, no black suits or flowers adorned the room and most importantly no awkward silences, hiding secrets.

Beth went to the kitchen and then returned to the living room. '*Shall we check upstairs*?' she asked; Sarah found herself in the centre of the room, unable to move.

'*Sarah?*' Beth gently encouraged and it jolted her into motion. '*Let's go upstairs, eh?*'

Sarah went ahead and walking into Steve's room

was difficult, undeniably difficult. She cried within seconds of entering and there was a lifetime of items spread out on the bed. Photographs lined up on units, a lot showing Steve and Sarah together. Musical equipment, personal belongings were dotted around and notes next to a few items where Jean was asking if she wanted any as keepsakes.

Beth placed her hand around Sarah's shoulders and whispered it was good to let it out, but Sarah shook her head *'No, it's like I don't know this room, this person ... I don't know why I'm crying really. I've wasted so much time, just working, not living; I don't want anything'*

Sarah turned towards the door *'Let's go'*. Beth glanced back around the room before following Sarah out and back down the stairs.

'Are you sure?' she checked but Sarah wiped her eyes. She was certain.

Voices in the distance met them at the bottom of the stairs and through the living room they could see Jean walking through the garden towards the kitchen door.

She wasn't expecting visitors before lunch and as the door opened a small boy run ahead and made his way to a kitchen cupboard.

'Wait, wait' Jean called after him, her voice full of laughter as she came up behind him and helped him with the door. *'Just one'* she giggled, and his little hand pulled out a mini bag of cookies.

'*What do you say*?' she asked him, then bending down she tapped her cheek and asked for a kiss. '*Thank you, Nanny,*' he said.

Jean jumped as she noticed two shadowy figures in the living room and pulled the little boy closer to her side.

'*Sarah*?' her tone higher than usual.

'*Nanny?*' Sarah echoed.

Jean instantly looked down at the little boy who was looking back at her. His brown wavy hair and rosy cheeks gave Sarah the answer to her question.

'*Steve's?*' Sarah asked, her voice breaking, Beth trying to hold her tight.

Jean started to sniffle, her voice struggling to remain calm, so she coughed and cleared her throat a couple more times.

'*What's your name*?' asked Beth. The boy hadtucked himself behind Jean's skirt and her hand lay on his head, her fingers wrapped in curls.

'*This ... is ... Stanley*' mumbled Jean. '*Steve's son*' she confirmed. Stanley looked up to his Nanny, then Beth. '*I'm 5*' he said. Sarah was still looking at the little fella, his ruddy complexion identical to Steve.

'*Steve was a Father*?' She continued. '*All those years I wanted a child, and he was already a Father*?!' Beth tugged at Sarah's blouse and whispered her name in hope of reminding her that there was a startled young boy in the room and this was not the time.

Jean nodded tearfully and explained only she had been involved in Stanley's life, not Steve; something she could not bear to admit. Steve had been quite flippant when the pregnancy was announced and when he found out the pregnancy was going ahead; he swore he would have nothing to do with it.

Jean hoped that he would do the right thing in time and although Steve would send money (more to keep the woman from knocking at Sarah's door, Beth decided), Jean could not allow this innocent child to grow up thinking he was not loved by his Grandmother. She hoped as he got older Steve would have more in common with him and always, always, pleaded with him to tell Sarah, as one day the truth would come out.

Sarah was still staring at Stanley. '*The woman from the funeral*?' she asked. Jean confirmed it was, she wasn't a bad person, just found herself in an impossible position. She was unsure whether to let Jean be part of Stanley's life considering Steve's denial, but Jean had been persistent, and the lady had been persuaded that Stanley had the right to know his family. She never expected Steve to leave Sarah or be any more involved in Stanley's life.

Sarah sat down as Beth made her way towards the

little boy who was smiling, with biscuit crumbs down his top and a little chocolate chip sitting in the corner of his mouth. Beth picked it off his lip and pretended to eat it, which made him laugh.

Jean walked over to Sarah and with tears streaming down her face she begged Sarah to see her predicament. To Sarah's surprise Jean swore when she spoke of Steve, saying he was selfish and she was embarrassed that she had raised a man who could not own up to his responsibilities and that both Sarah and Stanley deserved better.

Sarah raised her head, her cheeks white with shock, her heart heavy with pain; longing to be a mother. Yet now a stark reminder that her dream was never going to come to fruition. He didn't even acknowledge the child he had, in fact he was cold and unloving enough to deny his existence.

'I'm glad he's gone' Sarah said and stood up sharply, Jean rising alongside her.

'Forgive me?' Jean begged.

Sarah looked Jean in the eyes, then clasped her hands and pulled her close. They hugged momentarily and Sarah pulled back saying there was nothing to forgive.

'You were a good mother' she told her *'and you'll be a wonderful grandmother Jean. He's a lucky little boy and you can be proud of him. Let the world meet him. Show him off … I don't care who sees. He shouldn't be a secret!'*

Jean cried out loud, relief and freedom had taken its toll. *'Thank you my darling'*

Jean held out her hand and Stanley ran to her, clasping her leg as he did, giggling. *'Hello Stanley,'* said Sarah. *'Hello'* he replied.

'Only Julie next door knew' Jean told her. *'I have been getting looks from others in the street these past few days; up until now I have had to visit him, but now I won't hide him away anymore'.*

Sarah told Jean she didn't want anything from upstairs, she signed the necessary paperwork and collected a couple of coats and some wellington boots, before hugging Jean goodbye and wishing her lots of love for the future. There was something warming about knowing Jean had Stanley to fill the void in her life and little Stanley would now be able to know his dad and have a past to share, undoubtedly portrayed by Jean in a better light than he deserved.

Meanwhile, Jack arrived at George's house, in time to see his brother Charles leaving.

'They finally let you out' he joked. George's face lit up when Jack entered the room and he made himself comfortable in the armchair close by.

George adjusted himself, complaining that he felt well enough to leave Hospital so he shouldn't be confined to sitting in bed all day, but he accepted Jack's advice when it was given.

'Just give it a little time' Jack grinned. *'Perhaps you're missing Hospital food?'*

'Err no' George laughs, *'Mind you, the house kept me fed, so I did better than most'*

The Nurse in the next room popped in and told George she would return tomorrow, then with meds done, she reminded him to stay in bed for at least 24 hours.

Then a silence filled the room and George looked at Jack, who wondered whether this was the right time to talk openly. He was only too aware that George could do without any shocks right now but it's wasn't long before George invited him to talk candidly.

Jack looked down and fiddled with his watch. *'Come on'* George beckoned. *'Talk to me'*

Jack sighed and looked into the eyes of the man he respected so dearly.

'I've just had a conversation with mother' he began. George stayed quiet. *'Please tell me it's not true?'*

George paused, his eyes were watering and his breath laboured. To Jack's surprise he looks wounded, so he places his hand on top, by way of reassurance.

'*You, ok?*' he checked. George whispered he was, then apologised for not being able to speak up before. '*It wasn't my secret to share*' he continued.

Jack sat back once more and run his fingers through his hair, his eyes wide and face full of anguish.

'*No ….*' He begged. '*It has to be a mistake?*' he pleaded.

George again apologises, but Jack continues to rant. '*He was never a father to me … always difficult. Why the hell did he marry my mother if he wanted someone else?*'

Jack rose to pace around the bed and over to the window but George frowned, then asked Jack to tell him what he knows '*Tell me exactly*' he adds.

Jack reels off the information he was given, how his father had been pressured into marrying his mother, had been in love with a lady who gave birth to a daughter, after they married. The house knew, his mother found out years later and finally, that George had been given the burden of keeping their secret; and that the locket was a gift, delivered on behalf of his father.

George adjusted his position once more, then Jack attended to his pillows.

Jack was still waiting for an explanation and finally George agreed. '*Right*' he said. '*Anything else?*' Jack's quizzical look made for a change in

George's questioning, '*No, sorry. Let me explain*' he said.

George confirmed the information was true. His father was born of a time where duty came above everything else and to do the right thing, he knew Jack could never truly understand, but times were different and he impressed on Jack to find some empathy.

Jack returned to his seat and looked up at George, his gaze desperate. But sadly, this time George was unable to reassure the young man he had nurtured and had feared one day he would be called upon to explain.

'*George, I'm falling for her*' he implored. George's eyes widened and his head slowly shook to gesture '*no*'.

'*Jackson, please think about your mother*' he begged. '*Sarah is wonderful, she stole my heart on the first day – pretty, vulnerable and in need of rescuing. All the things any red-blooded male would want … but not you, it can't be you?*'

'*We spent the night together*' Jack confessed and with that George rested back into the plumped pillows and sighed aloud.

'*My niece!*' Jack snapped but this time his voice raised and started to recount their meeting, how they had been brought together and asking why no-one thought to tell him as soon as they knew? George tried in vain to explain that it was only when Sarah joined them for dinner that the truth came to light; what were the chances of their ever meeting?

He knew years ago that the baby, Sarah's Mother, had left the Cove and her Grandmother Ellie had encouraged it, hoping her daughter would never know the truth. It was his Lordship that took the news badly and unfortunately the boys didn't benefit from the unhappiness that prevailed.

'I did my best to be a good substitute' George said. *'I wanted you to know love and pride Jack, both you and Charles deserved his time, but I couldn't get him to realise he had so much more to lose'*

George tapped the bed and asked Jack to remain calm and pay attention.

'I know what we're asking Jack' he continued. *'But if not for yourself, what about Sarah? She has been through so much, so think about how she will feel when she finds out that her mother was abandoned, that her Grandmother dealt with the shame that fell on her family, caused by yours?'*

Jack stared forward, unable to blink, to think, or speak. He had never been in love and even before he could declare such, he was facing heartbreak.

Sarah would have to believe it was his decision, she trusted him, had opened up emotionally and he told her he would support her and be here when she returned, so what now? He desperately tried to contain his emotions, but released a muffled sound that George would never forget.

He pulled the sheet to his face and covered his eyes and George placed his hand on his head and whispered '*sorry*'

∞ ∞ ∞

Beth drove Sarah to her flat and pushing open the door they were surprised to see how empty it was. Sarah's clothes and belongings were still in place but everything else had been sorted; no bedding on the bed, or towels in the bathroom.

The kitchen was untouched and Beth asked if she could take some things, if Sarah was to walk away.

Jean would return the following week to arrange collection for a local charity, so it was now or never.

Sarah couldn't stop thinking about Stanley and had texted Jack on the drive over saying he would not believe the latest drama; Jack did not reply, for fear of his fingers texting '*ditto*'

There was something therapeutic about decluttering your life, in all ways. Now packing a couple of suitcases and pulling the door on yet another part of it, Sarah looked at Beth and smiled.

'*You're doing great*' Beth praised and the two managed a little chuckle as they headed to the car.

'*Not sure how I will manage all of this on the train*' Sarah said, so Beth suggested they leave some of it behind.

'*I will find a free weekend and bring it to you*' she grinned.

'*Sounds good to me*' Sarah agreed.

That evening Sarah tried texting Jack again, saying she was having a wobble and hoped he was alright? This time she received a smiley face emoji and a kiss and a brief update about George being home, which put her mind at ease.

The day had certainly thrown up surprises and unlike Sarah's first concerns of doom and gloom on the journey here, she felt incredibly lifted. Thoughts of Stanley initially cut through her but on reflection it cemented the fact that Steve was not the man for her, he had shown himself to be a poor father and partner, so with the benefit of hindsight, she had had a lucky escape.

Chapter Twelve

Waking early the following morning Sarah wondered what surprises were in store for her today and her fear was that the reading of the Will could uncover something else. She prayed to God for a smoother day.

Breakfast over, they drove to the Solicitors and found Jean waiting in the foyer. She looked happy to see Sarah and they embraced. Dan and Lois were in the waiting room and Sarah made her way in, followed by Beth, then Jean.

'*Hi*' Dan said as he rose from his seat. Lois stood alongside him, looking a little uncomfortable and unsure what to say.

Sarah on the other hand felt more at ease than she thought she would. She was quite accustomed to change now and this was just another step to rid herself of her past.

They only had a brief conversation before being invited into the room by the Solicitor.

'*Take a seat please*' he gestured to the group. Jean kept looking across at Sarah as the reading began.

Thankfully there were no surprises, no property to share and no real savings. Sarah was the beneficiary of Steve's life insurance; something she arranged and paid for herself. Dan was left the musical equipment and some of it would be worth selling which again Sarah said Dan could take with her blessing. She was happy to have nothing to do with it.

Jean mentioned Stanley but typically Steve had not mentioned his illegitimate son and the Solicitor flicked through pages, eventually having to ask who Stanley was; something that took Dan and Lois by surprise too. They in turn glanced at Sarah who jibed '*welcome to my world*'.

The meeting adjourned and Sarah rose first saying she would head off and although the small group were trying to talk amongst themselves, with Dan offering lunch, Sarah shook her head and declined and with that she left, with Beth hot on her heels.

She didn't look back once; the silence was deafening, broken only by the ding of the lift as the doors opened and they stepped inside.

When the doors closed Beth turned to Sarah and told her she did so well. '*Now it's your time*' she smiled. '*Damn right*' snapped Sarah.

Sarah texted Jack as Beth turned the car key – she sighed aloud and thanked Beth for being the best friend ever.

The evening gave cause for celebration. End of a life, start of a new and never did Sarah imagine it would have changed so much in such a short period of time.

She found herself talking about a future in the Cove, a life with Jack hopefully and as she spoke her face lit up, her eyes shone, and she giggled with joy. Beth couldn't help but laugh with her, it was intoxicating and liberating as she saw her friend release herself of everything that held her back. The future was certainly brighter.

Before closing her eyes, Sarah tried calling Jack but unfortunately her last memory was 2 missed calls? Then again, she hadn't thought of asking if he was working and she would see him soon enough.

Chapter Thirteen

T he following morning George was out of bed when the nurse arrived and although she tried to insist it was too soon, he would not hear of it. All he could think of was the pain he had brought upon Jack, asking him to give up on the woman he loved, and this was a cruel twist of fate knowing that time had asked the same of his Lordship, all those years before.

He told Jack things were different, but yet here they were ... the same being asked of the younger generation and if he had anything to do with it, he would do all he could to put things right.

The nurse was left with no choice but to assist

him and against her better judgement she agreed to drive him to see Lady Martha; after all, she had arranged for the private nurse to be on hand until George fully recovered.

However, the drive itself took it out of George, and he was a little out of breath as they arrived at the house. The large doors opened, and members of the household came to his aid. Finally, he found a resting spot by the fire in the drawing room and Lady Martha was notified of his arrival.

As she entered the room George attempted to rise but she gestured for him to stay sitting and made her way to join him, accepting the offer for tea as the door to the drawing room closed.

'George' she exclaimed. *'What are you doing here*?' Lady Martha wiped his brow with her handkerchief and noticed his obvious discomfort. *'You should be resting, bed rest'* she demanded.

George composed himself, then quietly spoke in earnest. *'We have to do something'* he started. *'Do what*?' she asked, her voice full of concern.

'Jack came to see me last night' George explained and with that, Lady Martha adjusted her position.

'Yes, I spoke with him, just as you suggested and it was the hardest thing I have ever had to do' she told him.

George tried to impress on her once more. *'Martha,*

please, I beg of you. We cannot have his happiness ruined by yet another secret?' he pleaded with her, but Lady Martha rose abruptly.

'It can't continue' she said sharply. *'She is his niece!'*

George steadied himself as he rose from his seat and stepping forward he gripped the mantlepiece for support. Lady Martha turned towards him, tears in her eyes praying George would understand her position.

'Is she though?' he dared to ask. The two stood close, locked in a gaze for a few seconds, their eyes searching frantically for the other to retreat.

Finally, Lady Martha drew breath and let out an exhausted sigh, pausing to look in the mirror ahead of them. It showed the elderly couple standing side by side, George now clutching her hand.

'There have been too many secrets Martha, but one word will silence me forever'

Lady Martha offered a brief smile, appreciating the sacrifice George had made for the family all these years. He married whilst in service and the two had been happy, but not before George and Lady Martha had grown close.

Many times the two had been affectionate with each other, whilst remaining faithful to their partners . One out of duty and one in the hope of true happiness. George had grown to care for his wife and although she was unable to have children, he was very fond of her.

He and Lady Martha had met in secret before he married and she always questioned whether George married to remove himself from temptation, something he later confirmed to be true.

He couldn't bear to see Lady Martha treated so coldly, unable to ease her pain or comfort her in the way he would like. Likewise, he had a duty to the family and whilst married, he would remain a gentleman; a vow was a vow.

Lady Martha turned and stared George directly in the eyes.

'Is he mine?' he asked.

'Why have you never asked before?' she put it to him.

'It wasn't right,' said George. *'He was your son and that was all I needed to remember. How could he ever know I may be his father?'*

George kissed the back of Lady Martha's hand and with that, she smiled, love still evident between them, after all these years.

'He was never like his Lordship' she went on. *'He surprised me over the years, always full of life, happy to help everyone. So, kind George, well ... you know that. So kind and caring'*

Lady Martha returned to her seat and sat down; George taking the opportunity of sitting close to her.

'*Is that why you stayed with us*?' she asked.

'*I wanted to stay close to you both*' George admitted. '*Home is where the heart is, after all*'

George sat forward and once again begged for her to reconsider.

'*If we don't tell him, we leave him broken hearted. Do you want that for him? Settling for someone else because he can't be with the one he loves?*'

Martha sipped her water. '*Of course, I don't*' she replied. '*We could have had a wonderful life together George*'. George agreed, adding that it wasn't too late for Jackson.

'*What about Charles*?' Lady Martha stopped herself in her tracks. '*… and the household?*'

George was relentless and not willing to give up now they had spoken the truth.

'*Charles is his father's son. He will judge both of us and then take his rightful place, but Martha, Jackson is not destined for grandeur. He is a Paramedic; he serves in a different way*'

Lady Martha shook her head and a tear appeared on her cheek, '*George, I can't do it!*'

George stood up, his breathing laboured and his tone firm. '*I have never asked anything of you Martha. Not to leave the life you had, not even to let me be the father I always wanted to be, but I am asking you now, for our son?'*

Lady Martha stared at George, the sacrifice etched on his face, pain still evident in their decisions to this day.

'*ok*' she spoke softly. '*For our son*'

Arrangements were made for them to talk with Jack the following day and a message was sent asking both the boys to join them for lunch.

Chapter Fourteen

The homecoming morning arrived, and Sarah squeezed Beth goodbye, thanking her profusely; with the two promising to make arrangements for a visit as soon as possible. Sarah also gave Beth a handwritten letter for the head teacher for the following week.

Sarah had spoken to the head and emailed to explain her circumstances and thanked her for being so understanding and such a great support during her time of need.

Now, finally, aboard the train for the last time, Sarah clutched her chest, holding her locket close to her heart and whispered to her mum that she loved her, and they were *going home* – for good.

A lengthy journey ahead, exhausted yet satisfied she had made the right decision, Sarah made herself comfortable and sent another message to Jack to say she had missed him and was looking forward to seeing him.

However, Jack woke with a different outlook. He

was troubled and had been drinking for most of the evening, eventually calling work to say he couldn't make his shift; something he had never done before.

How was he going to tell Sarah? He had wondered whether to drive to her late last night and speak to her face to face, so as to give her the opportunity of not returning to the Cove, if that was her preference?

She deserved to know that he had fallen for her, that this was out of his control, *but his niece*?!! He thought about opening another bottle but then a call from George sobered him up, perhaps there was hope? He agreed for lunch and arranged for his brother Charles to pick him up, on route.

Charles arrived with Cynthia and they had to knock a few times to get Jack's attention as he had fallen asleep in the chair.

'Good grief brother' Charles barked. *'What the hell happened to you?'* Jack gave a scornful glare as he fell onto the Jag's back seat.

Cynthia tutted and told him he needed a shower, but Jack ignored them both as they pulled away.

Charles tried again *'Heavy night*?' he asked, and this time Jack grunted '*something like that'*

Cynthia swivelled round, her hair swept up and a shiny pair of earrings flashed in the light. *'Still seeing that girl?'* she sniped, but in a manner that disgusted her. Jack sat back in his seat and looked the other way. '*Ok, then, girl trouble*' Cynthia remarked. The couple gave each other a sideways glance, but neither had ever seen Jack in such a state before.

When the boys arrived at the house, they were asked to wait in the drawing room and Cynthia was asked to wait alone in the sitting room, much to her disgust.

'*What's wrong*?' questioned Charles, as his huge stature stood firmly in the doorway. '*Please come in*' gestured George.

'*Are you feeling better*?' Charles touched his shoulder as they passed. '*Yes, healing well, thank you*' George replied.

Charles greeted his mother and took his place on the largest sofa. Jack shook George's hand, then offered a kiss to his mother who reeled in surprise at his condition. She held her mouth briefly as he breathed fumes into her face. '*Jackson*' she murmured. '*Let's get you some coffee*'

With that, drinks were brought to the room and Lady Martha's hand shook as she collected hers.

'*Mother*?' queried Charles, now a little concerned.

'*I'm fine, really I am*' she assured them and glanced a few times to George, as they prepared to explain.

George waited patiently for Lady Martha to start

the conversation, hoping to assist her where required but an hour or so passed with small talk, discussions about the estate and business, where it was obvious to George and Jack that she had never shown much interest.

Eventually, lunch was served, and Charles asked if Cynthia could join them; reminding his mother that she had been alone now, for over an hour.

To George's surprise Lady Martha apologised and agreed she could join them for lunch, adding they had something to discuss in private afterwards, so Cynthia would have to vacate the room once more when lunch was over.

Sarah was getting closer to home. The sun shone brighter and she found her thoughts centred around Jack. All she wanted was to get back to his reassuring arms and see what their future held.

She opened another bottle of water and started to drink; too much red wine last night she thought, but then she realised she hadn't felt 100% for a few days. Mind you, that was to be expected when you consider the complete rollercoaster her life had become of late.

Taking out her diary Sarah studied the dates and for a moment time stood still. She had missed her period? But then grief could cause such a delay. Then the realisation that when she slept with Jack she had not been prepared, they had talked about the fact that they had not used protection and the irresponsibility of their actions but all that was pushed aside after, because if Sarah was to become pregnant well, for her, it would be the icing on the cake!

But would Jack be happy with that? She had to snap herself out of such nonsense!

It was too soon to panic though, so if no sign in a few days she would take a test and he would be none the wiser, until she had something real to declare.

∞∞∞

Jack struggled with eating anything at all, choosing to sip water and pick at his food. He apologised to his mother, saying he knew she would understand; something Charles found odd. But Cynthia was on the case and kept nudging for information, asking if he had fallen out with Sarah, though she called her *'what's-her-name'* and only corrected herself when George said it out loud AGAIN.

Lady Martha was fully aware of her son's troubles and tried her best to keep the conversation flowing, along with George who so ardently filled in awkward silences. The two showed such strength in keeping a united front and were as tight as any fortress, but later they would be battling alone.

As lunch came to an end George suggested Cynthia made herself comfortable in the sitting room, adding Charles would join her shortly. With yet another disgruntled look Cynthia took her leave and pulled the heavy doors behind her.

Lady Martha apologised for what she was about to say and upon realising the conversation ahead, Jack put a halt to it.

'Mother, we agreed' he interjected, but Lady Martha raised her hand.

'No Jack, there's much more to it and in the circumstances you both need to know'. Charles spun round to look at his brother, then back to Lady Martha and finally George.

'Well, will someone tell me something?' he snapped impatiently.

George began and Lady Martha nodded, adding small sentences where she could. This was far too painful for her to repeat.

'So, let me get this right' he said, standing quickly and pushing his chair back with force. He pointed to Jack sitting to his left.

'Sarah is a product of father's affair with her grandmother Ellie; she had a baby girl who grew up and left the area. Her daughter … Sarah … then shows up in our lives … what? By chance?'

'*Hold on*' Jack barked. '*What are you insinuating*?*' Charles turned to his brother once again. '*Seriously brother, you have been played. She wants a piece of the pie!*'

Jack grabbed Charles by the scruff and pulled him in, his breath strong of liquor and his slurred words causing spit to hit Charles' face.

'*Stop!*' screamed Lady Martha. '*Jackson, stop!*' George rose up from his seat, trying to steady himself on the table. '*Charles, you have it wrong*' he bellowed, but it was enough to halt proceedings.

Jack released his brother, who scoffed at his choice in women. '*Prize loser brother!*' he jibed as he marched around the table to the window.

'*Charles, you're missing the point*' Lady Martha tried to gain control of the room. '*Please, both of you, allow me to explain. This is the most difficult conversation I will ever have with you. I too have carried pain throughout the years; don't I deserve to be heard?*'

Charles looked over at his mother and Jack returned to his seat.

George stood calmly, offering his hand to Lady Martha and encouraged her to take her seat, once more.

'*Ok, please listen to me*' George pleaded. Charles pulled a chair opposite to Jack at the table.

'*All ears George, my man!*' he said, smugly.

George took a deep breath.

'Your father did not have an affair. He loved Ellie when they were younger, but duty called and his father insisted he marry money and your mother's family proved suitable. Your father was broken hearted. I knew the young passionate man he was and it changed him, I'm telling you. Your mother was an innocent party in all this; again, doing what was expected by her family, so they were married. It was later we found out Ellie was pregnant, and a baby girl was born' George steadied himself, then looking at Martha; he continued.

'He asked me to take a design to the jeweller for Ellie's 30th birthday and it was the last keepsake she would accept; a locket which had a photo of Ellie and their baby. That is when I realised Sarah was related as she wore the locket to dinner. She did not know then, nor does she now!'

He looked at Charles who was presently silent, but he could see his judgmental mind trying to find a way back for Sarah to have a hidden agenda.

'Have you bedded her?' Charles called out to his brother. Jack slowly raised his eyes and a hatred crossed his face. *'You have … awesome!'*

George banged the table and all eyes returned to him. *'Charles, enough'* he said. *'Jackson is as innocent as Sarah and the two want to be together'* But before George could finish Charles butted in once more *'She's, our niece!'* he proclaimed. *'Is that why you've been on a bender*?'

Jack rose up and stormed away from the table; his mother close behind him. '*Please Charles, for once in your life, listen!*'

Charles poured himself another drink and then another '*Go on*' he instructed George.

Lady Martha gestured to Jack to sit back down and this time he placed himself next to his mother, at the head of the table. She chose to stand instead and asked George to take a seat.

'*My turn*' she said. '*I hope you can forgive me*'

The boys looked at each other, then to George for direction, but he lowered his eyes.

'*My marriage was cold, loveless you could say, though I always hoped your father would find time for me … or grow fond of me. He certainly made me feel that his life with me, stopped him being with her*' she sighed and reached for her handkerchief, dabbing her nose briefly.

'*Jackson, we have led you to believe you cannot be with Sarah because she is your niece. That is not true*' Jack darted a look in her direction, then to George who confirmed.

Charles also questioned that statement, then addressed them both.

'*You said father … *'. Lady Martha interrupted. '*Yes, she is **your** niece Charles, as stated*' then turning to Jack, she placed her hand over his and continued. *'But she isn't your niece Jackson, because he was not your father'* Jack's eyes widened, he had sobered up pretty quick by now; *'George is!'*

Charles stood once more, this time his chair fell to the floor, behind him.

'If you weren't a sick old man, I would knock you through the wall' he threatened George. *'and I would let you'* George replied, calmly.

Jack still silenced by the news, was looking at George, then his mother's cry pulled him to comfort her.

'We loved each other' George told them. *'We too were forbidden, so I stayed on at the estate to be close to you all'* Now he was looking at Jack who let go of his mother and looked over at George, a man he had respected and loved all these years.

'Your son?' he echoed, then looking back at his mother, the realisation that Sarah was not related to him, caused the broadest smile to appear on his face.

'So, Sarah and I ...?' Lady Martha nodded, stifling tears.

'Yes, you are free to be together' Jack grabbed her roughly and pulled her into his chest, causing her to let out a brief squeal of delight.

'I love you so much' he whispered. *'I love you too'* she told him, holding on tight.

Charles was still pacing the room and George was

trying to reassure him.

'You are your father's son and will rightfully take over the estate Charles. Your actions now will show us what type of Lord you will be'.

Charles spun round and glaring back at his mother, then Jack, he slowly turned his attention towards George.

*'Oh, don't worry, I don't want the scandal to be local news George. Your indiscretion with my mother can stay hidden under the carpet; our little secret!' h*e snarled.

∞∞∞∞

Sarah was nearing the Cove and her heart was pounding. She had been a little concerned when Jack had not been forthcoming with messages or calls, but then she knew he had a busy work life, so it was important to keep things in perspective.

As the coach pulled into the Cove, it was all she could do to not push past the queue of holiday makers and locals trying to disembark.

One face not expected amongst her welcome party was that of Cynthia. What was she doing here Sarah wondered, then questioned who the un-lucky recipient could be?

As bags were handed out and crowds dispersed Sarah became aware that Cynthia was heading towards her with the broadest of smiles. She raised her sunglasses above her eyes and popped them onto her head, holding her coiffured hair in place.

'*Back for another holiday*?' she grinned. Sarah thanked the driver, then stepping on to the pavement she asked Cynthia what she meant by that?

'*You just breeze into the Cove, a pleasant surprise for everyone*' she said curtly and again Sarah's look of surprise caused her to smile, and a short burst of laughter followed.

'*Are you here for me?*' Sarah tried again. '*Oh, my dear girl, no ... just wanted to see for myself if it was true?*'

Sarah took her jacket off and placed it on top of the suitcase. '*Ok Cynthia*' she said, 'W*hat is this about?*'

Cynthia delighted in telling Sarah about the conversation she had overheard at the house, how his Lordship was in fact her grandfather, that her mother was the child born '*out of wedlock (bringing shame – huge shame) on the family*' she added with delicious technicolour. Then of course, the fact that her mother moved away which helped everyone until Sarah returned with the locket and that completed the puzzle '*... and finally darling, if you haven't already worked it out, Jack is your Uncle!*'

Sarah looked through Cynthia, unable to focus on her face, or hear the words that followed. What was this? How twisted was this woman? Sarah felt a wave of heat wash over her and found herself quickly turning away to be sick behind the bench.

'*Ooh, nasty*' Cynthia chuckled. '*Come on*' she chortled. '*you must have known something*?' she tried to convince Sarah.

Sarah made her way to the bench and sat down, the sea air not as refreshing as the first time she arrived.

She looked across the road and could see the beach, the beautiful rocks and up on high, the manor house.

'*It isn't true*?' she begged, looking to Cynthia to withdraw the statement, for some modicum of kindness to leave her lips, but to no avail.

'*Where did you hear that*?' Sarah asked. This time Cynthia crossed her tanned legs and leant back on the seat, her lips salivating as she repeated a few overheard sentences.

'*Lady Martha told Charles and Jackson that her late husband had loved another before they married, and a child had been born ... your mother*'

She stopped only to observe Sarah's reaction to the news, then cut deeper.

'*I heard Charles accuse Jackson of sleeping with his niece*' she quipped '*and I think he must have known that, as he was legless when we picked him up today. Definitely a guilty conscience, wouldn't you say?*'

Cynthia rose, '*So*' she finished '*my work here is

done' then before she left, she looked back over her shoulder *'That won't go down well with the locals; you may wish to buy a return ticket ... sharpish!'* she finished, defiantly.

Sarah tried to stand but her shaking legs gave way and forced her to stay seated a little longer.

So many thoughts were rushing through her mind and the need to talk with Jack was ever increasing, yet if he knew she was his niece? ... well, that was unforgivable.

The next hour passed without Sarah realising she had company. The bench started to fill, and others stood around the bus stop shelter, chatter filling the air.

'Heading home?' came an elderly voice. Sarah turned in slow motion to see a lady to her left, unable to hide the tears falling down her cheek. She was offered a tissue.

'Oh lovey' she oozed *'Holiday romance?'* Sarah still silent, took the tissue and wiped her eyes.

'Cads. All of them' she announced. *'Often the way. In fact, when we were young, we were warned; life was very different then and our parents would have none of it!'* she declared. She looked at her faithful companion Jim, standing by her side and he nodded silently.

'My father wouldn't even let us sit in the living room on our own, until we were married' she added.

'*Not like today*' she moaned. '*No, nowadays they can sleep with each other on the first date, then complain when they're left holding the baby!*'

Sarah blinked slowly, unable to answer, laugh or cry. '*Oh no, are you in the family way*?' she questioned and with that Sarah looked to the ground.

'*Hey, you'll be ok*' the lady comforted. '*You're made of strong stuff, you'll see*'

Jim pointed as the coach came up the hill and Sarah's new confidante, who introduced herself as Gladys, nudged her. '*Let's get you on board*' she suggested.

The coach started to fill, and mainly older couples boarded. Sarah was still sitting on the bench when Jim came back to assist her with her case. The driver was placing bags in the hold and called across to Jim to come over, so he bent down to Sarah and asked if he could assist her.

Sarah looked up at his kind face and managed a '*no thank you*' but then she heard her name being called, this time from afar. '*Sarah*' it came again and a little louder until she realised it was Jack running up the hill.

'*Yes please!*' Sarah hastily changed her mind and caught Jim's arm. He looked surprised but helped the driver load her case while Sarah quickly made her way up the steps. There was still movement on the coach with folk getting settled and then suddenly Jack was on board, frantically searching with his eyes.

'*Sarah?*' he called out once more and with that she tried to slip down behind a heavy-set woman, using her floppy sun hat as cover. Jack was confused and tried to pass a few passengers who were standing in the aisle, one placing a bag overhead and others removing outer garments, plus busying themselves with flasks and sandwiches for the journey. '*Wait a minute son,*' said another traveller.

Jack called out again for Sarah, but she remained quiet. '*Is that him?*' proclaimed Gladys. Sarah nodded.

'*She's going home*' Gladys informed him, much to Sarah's horror. Jack called down the coach once more. '*Sarah, please?*' he shouted.

'*Stop shouting son*' Jim requested. '*You're giving me a headache*'

Jack apologised and as the aisle became a little clearer, he could see the driver heading up the steps.

'*You on this trip?*' he asked but Jack shook his head and said he was just needing to speak to someone on board.

The driver said he only had a minute and looked down the bus, in hope of speeding things up.

'*Miss, do you wish to speak with this gentleman?*' he called out.

'*He's no gentleman!*' yelled Gladys. Sarah sunk down in her seat and hoped the driver would insist on Jack leaving, but he wasn't finished.

'*Sarah!*' this time Jack shouted even louder and when Jim asked him to once again refrain from doing so, he said he would not be getting off until Sarah answered him.

Now the aisle was clear, and Jack stepped forward, only to be blocked by a wooden walking stick and a glaring Gladys, holding on tight.

'*You are not invited*' she warned him and looking back at Sarah she said she was happy to get Jim to '*see him off*' if she wanted. Sarah was embarrassed enough by now and as the coach settled down and conversation came to a hush; there was nowhere to hide.

She raised herself up and looked at Jack. He still carried the bad night evidently and she could tell he was distressed. '*Talk to me*' he pleaded.

'*I need to go Jack, just let me go*' she whispered, hoping chatter would resume and they would not be overheard.

'*Come with me and we can talk*' Jack begged. Gladys once again tapped the walking stick and Jack acknowledged its presence.

'*I'm not moving*' he told her, '*Sarah, please don't go. Talk to me first and if you still want to leave, you can get the next one?*'

Sarah started to cry *'See what you've done!'* Gladys barked. *'You're all the same'* she continued. *'You promise the world, get them into bed and when they fall pregnant you lose interest'* Jack looked startled and Sarah gasped, holding her hands across her mouth. *'Pregnant?'* he stated, his face now breaking into a smile, *'but, that's wonderful'*

Gladys tapped the stick barrier once more *'Yeah, you say that now, but next summer you'll turn your head for another … you're all the same'*

Jack ignored her comments and with a gentler expression, he spoke softly and tried to encourage Sarah to talk with him, privately.

'I know' Sarah explained *'Cynthia told me'* Jack looked confused, then repeated her words *'Cynthia?'*

Sarah nodded, wiping tears away *'She was at the house when your Mother told Charles'*

Jack stepped back and had to steady himself on the head rest. *'No'* he said under his breath.

The driver called out to the passengers and caught Jack's attention. *'Time to decide, on or off'* he ordered, making his way back to the cab.

Jack called out to Sarah one final time and walked forward, only pausing as he reached the roadblock that was Gladys.

'She has it wrong' he tried in vain, but Sarah's upset turned to frustration.

'*Jack, your father had an affair with my grand-mother. My grandmother brought shame to her family and was forced to raise my mum on her own.*'

Gladys piped up '*See, that was what it was like in our day*'

Sarah continued '*We cannot be together Jack*' but Jack refused to listen and confessed she was wrong.

'*I'm your niece!*' she bellowed.

The bus fell silent, with gasps all around.

'*You scoundrel*' barked Gladys as she rose up from her seat, stick in hand. '*Go on, get off!*' she demanded but Jack had had enough and pushing the walking stick to one side, he made one last attempt to get Sarah's attention.

'*No, you're not, because George is my father*' Sarah fell back onto her seat with a thud as Jack crouched beside her. '*We are not related Sarah; George is my father, don't you see?*'

'*I love you*' he said. '*I want to be with you, here or wherever you want. I want to marry you, have a family with you ... but please Sarah ... get off this ruddy coach!*'

'*Oh*' muttered Gladys. '*Maybe he's not such a bad sort after all*' she mumbled. Jack flashed her a glare and they both smiled when they heard Jim tell her to be quiet '*for once in her life!*'

Jack helped Sarah off the coach and the driver

hurried to the side hatch to remove her case, complaining they were running very late now.

Finally, the coach pulled away and chugged off in the distance.

Jack pulled her close and they stood in silence for a moment; his heart pounding through his chest and Sarah's relief brought tears.

It took a little time for Jack to convince her that he spoke the truth, but finally Sarah pushed his hair from his eyes and accepted a kiss.

    '... s*omeone needs a shower'* she teased.

    '*There's room enough for two*?' he winked.

Sarah placed her hand on her stomach and squinted in the sunlight.

    '*What about three*?' she managed to whisper.

    '*Even better...*' he beamed.

The End

Synopsis

'Going home' is about hope and new beginnings, but mostly self-belief and empowerment.

Hurt and betrayal are very real emotions; but how we manage them is testament to who we really are, and in our lives, we are rarely tested to the full.

But even through heartbreak, we can overcome and live a truer version of ourselves. The shedding of pain can be empowering and it gives way to us having more of ourselves to offer.

Sarah's journey is certainly an eventful one and we begin with the day of her partner's funeral, where she finds herself aged 40 and single – a daunting prospect.

Her first instinct is to return home to Cornwall, a happier time in her life that she shared with her mother.

However, fate plays a hand in her journey and the summer presents her with more than she could ever have imagined.

Her mother used to say *'If it's meant for you, it won't pass you by'.*

Sarah needed to trust that now and believe in the impossible.

Acknowledgement

To my family and friends who have continued to support me, I thank you dearly.
From reading drafts, giving honest feedback and encouraging me to continue; all of you have brought me to this moment ... *so, I blame you* :)
Lastly, to my husband, for always believing in me. I love you x

Books By This Author

Finding Grace

A Missing Persons Series.
Finding Grace is the first, where we meet Sam and Jed, who play an integral part in a UK Missing Persons Bureau.
Sam finds herself in the terrifying position of her own grandchild, 2 yr old Grace, going missing.
Even with years of experience and resources to hand, Sam soon realises she is living every parents nightmare.

One More

The 2nd book takes a closer look at Jed; his past and in particular the dark road he has travelled.
This time he risks not only his life, but that of his family, as he searches for one more.
However, in doing so, he has to return to a place that haunts him still and Sam fears she will lose him.

Price To Pay

Our 3rd visit to the Bureau has Sam tested once more as she assists the Police with their investigation.

At first she welcomes the opportunity to play a part; in thanks for their continued support, but it soon becomes clear that she is deeper than any of them had imagined and for the first time, she understands Jed's world.

Printed in Great Britain
by Amazon

74543318R00102